BRUCE COVILLE

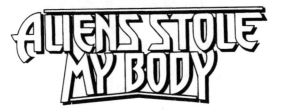

Books by Bruce Coville

The A.I. Gang Trilogy
Operation Sherlock
Robot Trouble
Forever Begins Tomorrow

Bruce Coville's Alien Adventures
Aliens Ate My Homework
I Left My Sneakers in Dimension X
The Search for Snout
Aliens Stole My Body

Camp Haunted Hills
How I Survived My Summer Vacation
Some of My Best Friends Are Monsters
The Dinosaur that Followed Me Home

Magic Shop Books
Jennifer Murdley's Toad
Jeremy Thatcher, Dragon Hatcher
The Monster's Ring

My Teacher Books
My Teacher Is an Alien
My Teacher Fried My Brains
My Teacher Glows in the Dark
My Teacher Flunked the Planet

BRUCE COVILLE

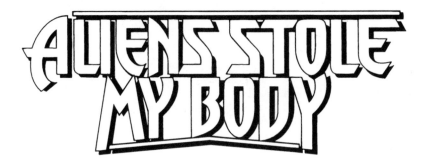

ALIENS STOLE MY BODY

Illustrated by
Katherine Coville

A MINSTREL® HARDCOVER
PUBLISHED BY POCKET BOOKS
New York London Toronto Sydney Tokyo Singapore

A MINSTREL HARDCOVER

 A Minstrel Book published by
POCKET BOOKS, a division of Simon & Schuster Inc.
1230 Avenue of the Americas, New York, NY 10020

Text copyright © 1998 by Bruce Coville
Illustrations copyright © 1998 by Katherine Coville

ISBN: 0-671-02414-0

First Minstrel Books hardcover printing August 1998

10 9 8 7 6 5 4 3 2 1

A MINSTREL BOOK and colophon are registered trademarks of Simon & Schuster Inc.

Printed in the U.S.A.

For
Justin John Bonafide,
most loyal of fans,
who has already gone on to the next adventure

CONTENTS

Contents

A Note from Bruce

A long time had passed since I last heard from
Rod Allbright, and I was beginning to get worried. So I was relieved when I came into my office
last week and found a package from him, describ-
ing his latest adventures.

I've never actually met Rod, you understand.
But he occasionally sends me one of these packages. They always arrive under mysterious circumstances, and without explanation. That is, I
leave the office at night, locking the door as
usual—and the next morning I find a manuscript
on my desk.

(If only it was always that easy!)

I'm not sure, exactly, why Rod has chosen me
to receive these packages. My guess is that it's
because I had already developed a reputation for
writing books about aliens before his own adventures started. So I probably seemed like a natural
person to bring these stories to. Or maybe it's
just because we live in the same area. Whatever
the reason, it's clear that these stories can only

be published as *fiction*, since the League of Worlds is not yet willing to admit to us Earthlings that it actually exists.

If you haven't read any of Rod's previous adventures, there are a few things I should tell you before you plunge into this one.

Rod first got tangled up with the Galactic Patrol when the good ship *Ferkel* accidentally landed in a vat of papier-mâché he was making. The ship's captain, Grakker, enlisted Rod to help the crew catch a vicious little villain named BKR (you pronounce it "Bee Kay Are"), the cruelest being in the galaxy.

After that adventure was over, Rod figured he had seen the last of the aliens. But that summer he and his cousin Elspeth were kidnapped into Dimension X by a huge orange monster named Smorkus Flinders. The monster was using Rod as bait to get Grakker and his crew. And, indeed, the crew did come to rescue him—though by the time that adventure was over, it would be hard to say who rescued whom.

It was at this point that Rod discovered his own missing father was also an alien. Known to the greater galaxy as Ah-rit Alber Ite, years earlier he had been working with BKR on a scientific breakthrough. But when he discovered that BKR was actually trying to build the most terrible weapon ever imagined, Ah-rit fled to Earth, taking with him the key bit of information BKR needed to finish the weapon.

After arriving on Earth, Ah-rit Alber Ite lived quietly for several years under the name Arthur Allbright. He married, and had three children, Rod being the oldest. When BKR finally figured out where Ah-rit was hiding he came after him. For the sake of the universe, Ah-rit fled once again. But before he left, he took the secret information out of his own head and stored it in Rod's brain, thinking this would make it even harder for BKR to find it.

After a series of wild adventures, Rod finally caught up with his father, only to learn that Ah-rit wasn't quite as alien as he had been told. His father was actually from ancient Atlantis and had left Earth 35,000 years ago. (Ah-rit had spent a lot of the time since then in suspended animation, which is why he doesn't seem anywhere near his age.)

Unfortunately, no sooner had Rod and his dad reconnected than BKR showed up again. In order to save his father, Rod agreed to surrender to BKR. But unknown to BKR, before the swap was made, Snout, the Master of the Mental Arts, emptied the contents of Rod's brain into the large (and largely unfilled) brain of Seymour the chibling, a strange creature from Dimension X to whom Rod was psychically bonded.

That worked just fine as far as saving the universe goes. But it left Rod without a body of his own.

As you can imagine, he was less than happy with this situation.

As for what happened next—well, I'll let Rod tell you that in his own words, in the pages that follow.

I'll be back next time I hear from Rod. Until then, keep your eyes on the stars. And always remember Galactic Law Number One: Be Kind!

Your friend,

Bruce Coville

BRUCE COVILLE

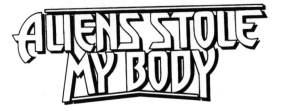

CHAPTER
1

My Dangerous Brain

IT WAS HARD TO DECIDE WHAT WAS THE WORST PART about not having a mouth—not being able to eat, or not being able to talk.

It wasn't like I was going to starve; Edgar, the other half of the two-part alien creature my brain patterns had been merged with, was beaming energy into "our" body. But I missed the pleasure of tasting things, of chewing and swallowing. After all, I had been doing it for twelve years (doing a lot of it, actually, which was why I used to be slightly pudgier than I would have liked). So eating had gotten to be a real habit with me.

Talking, which you also need a mouth to do, wasn't quite as much of a habit. (I had started eating at least a year earlier than I had started talking.) Even so, I had some important things I wanted to say, and not having a mouth made it a lot harder.

Though I found this personally inconvenient, it was just as well for the world at large, since my brain happened to contain the secret for making a bomb that would destroy Time itself, freezing everyone in the universe in a state of total despair.

This information being in my brain probably wouldn't have mattered much (heck, I hadn't even known it was there myself until a couple of days earlier) except for one problem: BKR, the cruelest being in the universe, was after it. That was why he had stolen my body—to get at the information in my brain. So transferring the contents of my brain out of my body had saved the universe. Which was all fine and good, except it left me stuck sharing the body of a six-legged, one-eyed, no-mouthed creature named Seymour, who also happened to be a major wise guy.

It was no picnic, let me tell you—and not just because I couldn't eat fried chicken.

To make things worse, Seymour and I were always fighting. Not because we didn't like each other. The problem was we just couldn't get away from each other, no matter what we did. We both had a growing fear that we would be stuck this way forever. Whenever I started grumbling about it, Seymour would reply, *Look, Uncle Rod, this is no bed of roses for me, either. Love it or leave it!*

Bruce Coville

Unfortunately, leaving was easier thought than done.

So we were already in a bad mood when Captain Grakker called the crew of the *Ferkel* together for a meeting that ended up making us even crankier.

With Edgar-the-furball riding on our shoulder, we joined the other members of the crew in the ship's main meeting room. I noticed that the aliens had shrunk my father to half his normal height, which made him almost as short as them. This was just as well, since it also made it easier for him to fit into the room. Elspeth (my annoying little stowaway cousin) was her normal height, which made her a few inches shorter than my shrunken dad. As for Seymour and me, we came up to everyone's knees.

Sometimes I felt like the family dog.

Grakker called the meeting to order. He had a head like a hairless gorilla—well, a hairless gorilla with green skin and a pair of nubby little horns sprouting from its forehead. His brick-red uniform fit tight to his bulky, muscular body. He was incredibly cranky. Even so, I had become very fond of him during our adventures together.

As soon as everyone had settled in, Grakker growled, "It is time to decide on our next course of action."

"Well, we go get Rod's body, of course," said Elspeth. "That should be obvious."

3

I appreciated the sentiment. Even so, as a stow-away, Elspeth didn't really belong at the meeting, so she shouldn't have been speaking out—especially not before anyone else had a chance to talk. But the mere fact that she *shouldn't* do something had never stopped my cousin before, so there was no reason to expect it to slow her down now.

"It's not that simple," said Grakker, glaring at Elspeth from under his heavy green brow. "We are still in renegade status. Now that the immediate threat to the universe is over, the most appropriate thing for us to do is return to Galactic Headquarters and surrender ourselves for proper discipline."

"You're out of your mind!" cried Elspeth. "What did you do, Madame Pong? Slip the 'Demented Ding-Dong Module' into his skull?"

This was the first time I was actually glad I didn't have a mouth, since laughing would have been a big mistake. Elspeth, for a wonder, immediately realized she had gone too far. Of course, given the look on Grakker's face, a blind man sitting behind a closed door on the other side of the planet probably could have figured that out.

Anyway, that was why Elspeth got thrown out of the meeting.

Once Elspeth was gone—and she didn't go quietly—Tar Gibbons requested permission to speak.

Tar Gibbons is the *Ferkel*'s Master of the Martial Arts, and also my special teacher. It (you don't call the Tar "he" or "she"—that's offensive) has a lemon-shaped body, four legs, and enormous eyes. The Tar had invited me to be its *krevlik*, which is kind of like an apprentice, while we were in Dimension X. Since then, it had taught me amazing things. I loved the Tar very much. There is nothing better than having a true teacher.

"The thing is," said the Tar, craning its long neck forward, "even though the danger is over for the moment, that situation will not necessarily persist. After all, it will not take long for BKR to realize that while he has Rod's body, the information stored in Rod's brain is not there, since that brain is now completely empty. Once BKR realizes that, it is likely he will come looking for young Deputy Allbright. Warrior Science tells us it is better to meet the enemy than to let him seek us out. Therefore, I suggest we try to determine which direction BKR will go, then beat him to it."

"Your plan is a good one, noble warrior," said my father, speaking for the first time.

Seymour and I turned our one big eye in Dad's direction. He was a lean man, with a thick head of dark brown hair and a bushy mustache. Except for his eyes, he didn't look anywhere near 35,000 years old.

I was still amazed that we had actually found him. I mean, he had disappeared nearly three years before—just run off on our family, I had always thought. That was before I discovered he was actually an ancient Atlantean, and a semi-alien.

Talk about having a secret life!

Now, you would think that after crossing thousands of light-years and traveling right into the belly of an ancient stone beast to find my father, I could have had a little while to enjoy the fact that we were together again. But no— I hadn't even had an hour with him before Snout, the Master of the Mental Arts, had poured the contents of my brain into Seymour's belly (which was where *his* brain was located). Okay, so Snout did it to save the universe. Even so, it was annoying that instead of being father and son, Dad and I were now more like father and pet.

I couldn't even talk to him, since I no longer had a mouth. Fortunately, Seymour and I *could* communicate mentally with Snout, who would then speak our words aloud so that we could be included in conversations. The frustrating thing was, while Snout could "open a line" into our head, we weren't able to do the reverse. It was like being locked in a house with a telephone that only took incoming calls—and then only from one person.

So the only way I could communicate with Dad was through Snout.

This was not a situation that led to long, private chats.

Fortunately, Snout had opened a connection with Seymour and me as soon as the meeting started. I could always tell when he had made contact. It wasn't like he actually said anything into our head, no *Line open, ready to receive!* kind of message. It was simply that I could sense his mind touching ours. It's hard to explain the change, other than to say it was like noticing the way the light feels on your skin when the sun comes out from behind a cloud.

I was about to ask Snout to say that I agreed with Dad and Tar Gibbons about going after BKR when the ship's diplomat, Madame Pong, spoke up. Her yellow face was serious as she said, "Grakker's intention to return to Galactic Headquarters is wise and appropriate. The Tar's suggestion that we seek out BKR also has great merit. But there is a third point that must be considered: We must, at all costs, keep Rod's brain and the information it contains away from BKR. Therefore, Rod should not be on the ship if it goes in search of BKR." She paused, then added, "I think Rod wants to say something."

She probably figured this out from the way Seymour and I were standing on our hind legs and waving four little blue paws in the air.

Tell them I have to go after BKR, I thought to Snout.

I will tell them, he replied, *but I do not think they will agree.*

He was right, of course. My father shook his head and said, "Listen, Rod. I understand that you see this as personal between you and BKR. But if he gets his hands on the information I stored in your brain, it could mean the end of life as we know it for everyone in the universe. We simply cannot afford to let you anywhere near the little beast."

Maybe you should just kill me, I thought bitterly.

Though I had not intended him to, Snout spoke the words out loud.

"That would probably be the wisest thing to do," said Tar Gibbons.

Dad shot the Tar a ferocious look.

"I didn't say I was recommending it," said the Tar, stretching its long neck forward. "I was simply pointing out that there is a degree of wisdom in the idea. Rod's brain is, after all, a menace to the universe. However, Rod is my *krevlik,* and I will fight to the death anyone who tries to harm him."

Phil the Plant, our technical officer, waved his

tendrils to indicate he had something to say. Well, something to burp, actually, since he talks by burping air out of the pods that hang from his stems.

Grakker pointed to him.

Phil spread his leaves. I could see his little symbiote, Plink, clinging to his stem. The plant burped once, to clear his pods. Then he made the most horrifying suggestion I could imagine.

CHAPTER
2

The Beast's
Dangerous Belly

"WE HAVE THREE DIFFERENT THINGS THAT NEED TO BE done," burped Phil. He ticked them off on his leaves. "First, we need to pursue BKR to regain Rod's body. Second, we need to hide Rod, so BKR can't get him. Third, we need to re-establish contact with Galactic Headquarters. Therefore, we should consider dividing into three groups."

No! I thought, so hard I was almost surprised that the others couldn't hear me. *We're a crew! We have to stick together.*

I could tell Grakker felt the same way. His eyes bulged, and he made a strangled sound in his throat. But he didn't say anything, which let me know that even though he *felt* the same way, he also thought Phil was right.

No one else spoke. Everyone looked at Grakker, waiting for him to decide.

"Phil makes a wise suggestion," said the captain at last. "I will take the *Ferkel* back to Galactic Headquarters—to surrender, and also to plead for mercy for my crew." He turned to my father. "Ah-rit Alber Ite, I suggest you use *your* ship to search for BKR."

"I believe that is a wise choice, Captain," said my father, bowing his head slightly. "Since I have worked with BKR, I may be able to track him more effectively. I know several of his hideouts and some of the people he has contact with. In fact, I suspect I know where he is heading right now. My hope is that since extracting the information from Rod's brain will be a delicate process, he won't attempt it until he gets to this particular lab, and that he will therefore be keeping Rod's body in suspended animation for the time being. If that's the case, he won't discover the switch for some time yet." Dad frowned. "Unfortunately, we can't count on this. While there is no valid reason for him to animate Rod's body, he might want him around just to torment. So we can't be sure how long the trick will work."

"I will go with Ah-rit," said Tar Gibbons. "This is a trip where Warrior Science may be important. However, Warrior Science also raises another issue."

"And that is?" asked Grakker.

"When BKR discovers the deception, he will renew his attempts to gain the information. Warrior Science tells us that when the enemy cannot reach us directly, it will sometimes attack those we love. Therefore, someone must be sent to guard Mrs. Allbright, lest BKR attempt to abduct her in order to get to Rod."

I felt a cold chill.

"I will tend to that," said Grakker. "As soon as we are away from the Mentat and on our way to Galactic Headquarters, I will send a message urging them to set a guard on the Allbright home. There should be enough ships in that sector to get one to Earth in a matter of hours, certainly no more than a day."

"That should be more than enough time," said my father. "Especially since I believe that BKR is currently heading *away* from Earth."

That was a relief—and about the only good thing to come out of the meeting so far. I was still stunned by the fact that my father and my teacher were both going to leave me.

"Then that is settled," said Madame Pong. "As for me, I think it wisest if I stay with Rod and Elspeth while these other missions are going on. Not, however, on the Planet of the Mentat. We need to find someplace obscure to hide."

"Perhaps this would be the best place anyway,"

said Tar Gibbons. "After all, BKR would hardly expect you to stay here waiting for him. So staying and waiting might be the wisest thing to do. Of course, he might think that we would think that, and decide to come here anyway. Or he might think that we would think that he thought that, and if we did think that then we would—" The Tar paused, squinched up its face, then said, "Oh, never mind."

Madame Pong smiled. "Actually, staying here might be a good idea, if not for the fact that I suspect there is a traitor in the Mentat."

"A traitor in the Mentat?" cried Snout in disbelief.

"I fear our diplomat is correct," said Tar Gibbons. "Otherwise, how to explain the escape of Smorkus Flinders so soon after we had handed him over to their authority?" It turned to Madame Pong. "I bow to your superior wisdom, good lady. Where do you have in mind?"

Madame Pong smiled. "Not long ago I promised Rod's mother we would take him to see the weeping forests of Kryndamar. Perhaps this is the time to make good on that promise—especially since Kryndamar is only a dimensional jump or two away. We don't want to delay those going after BKR any longer than necessary."

"Agreed," said Grakker. He turned to Snout. "And where will you go, Flinge Iblik?" he asked, using our Mental Master's formal name.

14

Snout was silent for a moment, his lizardlike purple face still and unreadable. Finally he said, "I am torn. I long to accompany my captain on his mission, to give him aid and support. I also desire to be part of the hunt for BKR. However, I think it is best if I forego both those choices and stay with Madame Pong's group. Otherwise, Rod will have no way to communicate."

"Then I shall accompany Captain Grakker," burped Phil. "After all, he needs *someone* to run the ship."

"I can run the *Ferkel* perfectly well," growled Grakker.

Phil waved a tendril at him. "It is not fitting for you to return alone, Captain."

"I am not a captain!" shouted Grakker. "I gave up that honor when I went against Galactic orders to go in search of BKR."

"You will always be Captain to us," said Madame Pong quietly.

Grakker blinked, and for a second I almost thought I saw his lip tremble. Then he said gruffly, "Do not make your crime any worse than it already is. Prepare the *Ferkel* for departure. Ah-Rit, I think it is best if you use your ship to take Rod and the others to Kryndamar."

And that was how the crew of the *Ferkel* divided into three parts.

As we left the meeting, I felt the way I did

after Dad had disappeared; I felt like I was losing my family.

Which made me wonder how Mom was doing back on Earth, with both me and Dad gone, and only the twins still at home. Even though Little Thing One and Little Thing Two (my pet names for the twins) had bugged me something fierce, I missed them like crazy.

Don't get sentimental! ordered Seymour. *With an eyeball like mine, if we start to cry, we'll probably get dehydrated.*

Sometimes I wanted to kick him. Of course, since I was inside his body, that would have hurt me as much as it did him. Besides, when it came right down to it, he had more control of the body than I did. That annoyed me, but was basically fair, since it really was his body, and I was only a visitor.

"Rod, come for a little walk with me, would you?" said Dad. "We need to talk." He turned to Snout and asked him to come, too.

Normally I would have been glad for an invitation like that. Since I had found Dad, I tried to be with him as much as possible. But I wasn't sure I wanted to talk to him right now. I was too mad.

What made things worse was that deep down inside I knew he was right; I *shouldn't* go on the quest for BKR.

The problem was, going after him was the thing I wanted most in all the world to do.

We left the *Ferkel*. This did not take us outside, exactly. We were deep underground, beneath the Mentat, the school where Mental Masters like Snout are trained.

Not only were we underground, we were actually *inside* the belly of an incredibly huge beast—a beast so vast and enormous its stony insides were like massive caverns. My father had helped create this beast, which gnawed ceaselessly at the roots of the great tree that housed the Mentat.

When I had asked Dad if the beast wouldn't destroy the tree of the Mentat, he had shrugged and said, "Perhaps. Perhaps not. For now, they are in balance. The tree grows, the beast gnaws, and everything stays the same."

Dad had retreated into the beast to hide from BKR when he realized what the little villain really intended to do with the project they had been working on together. Now Snout and Seymour and I followed him through a series of tunnels that led to the chamber where he kept his ship, the *Jean*. (He had named it in honor of my mother.)

As we walked, we heard a great thump—the beating of the beast's heart. According to Dad, the heart was a piece of living stone the size of our house back on Earth. Rather than blood, the beast had hot lava flowing through the rocky channels that made up its veins.

As we approached the *Jean,* we saw someone waiting nearby. It was Selima Khan, who had helped us escape from the dungeons beneath the Mentat. She looked like a female version of Snout. This wasn't surprising; the two of them were from not only the same planet, but the same egg group.

"Greetings, Flinge Iblik," she said now, using Snout's formal name.

"Greetings," replied Snout, making a hand gesture I had never seen before.

Selima Khan's eyes widened. She swept her cloak around her in a swirl of purple, threw her head back, and stalked off without another word.

Holy cow, what's wrong with her? asked Seymour—speaking inside my head, of course.

I don't have the slightest idea, I replied.

I wanted to ask Snout about it, but he had broken his contact with us.

We turned to the ship, and I studied it with pleasure. (One of the few good things about being stuck inside Seymour was that he had the most phenomenal eyesight you can imagine. I saw things more clearly, and in more detail, than I ever had before.)

The ship was sleek and powerful, and it pleased me that it belonged to my father.

The room we sat in to talk was very comfortable, not only physically but mentally—mostly because it looked more like the kind of place where I had grown up than anything on the *Ferkel* did. Dad's ancient Earth background, I guess.

"How you doing, son?" he asked, once we were all sitting.

I'm okay, I thought.

You are not, replied Seymour, even as Snout spoke the words out loud for me.

Seymour was right, of course; I wasn't okay, and we all knew it. I was terrified about what was going to happen, crushed because I was going to be separated from Dad again, and totally freaked out over being stuck in an alien body.

Dad sighed. "Rod, I wish things could be different."

So do I! I thought quickly.

If I had been doing my own talking, I might have kept that thought to myself. As it was, Snout repeated it before I could stop him.

"Well, I can't blame you for that," said Dad. He paused, sighed, then said, "Listen, son, I have some things I need to tell you. When I settled on Earth and married your mother, I thought it was going to be the end of my wanderings. Probably

I was fooling myself, which is the greatest error anyone can make—especially someone who is supposed to be a Mental Master. So I want to tell you I'm sorry. If I had known this would happen . . ."

He spread his hands helplessly. What could he say? That if he had known this was going to happen, he would never have married Mom . . . never have had me?

I thought about that for a second. Would I rather not exist than be in this situation? Absolutely not. I loved being alive.

I just wanted my body back.

"It's okay, Dad," I said, through Snout.

He smiled. "Look, Buster—I'm supposed to be reassuring you, not the other way around." He paused again, then said, "I thought you might like to see some pictures."

"What kind of pictures?"

"Sort of a . . . family album."

He touched a button. One of the walls turned into a viewing screen, showing three-dimensional images that looked so real I felt as if I could walk into them. And I did want to walk into them, because what Dad had to show me was a series of pictures of his hometown, ancient Atlantis. I loved seeing that strange and beautiful city, with its graceful towers and weird statues. What I loved even more were the pictures he showed me

20

of his family. After all, even though they had died 35,000 years ago, his parents were my grandparents; his brothers and sisters my aunts and uncles. It was good to see their faces. But it also left me wondering what it would have been like to grow up knowing them.

"This was my little brother, Kah-nath," said Dad, flashing a picture of a handsome young man of about twenty. He had bright red hair, and a quizzical expression that made you think he was interested in everything in the world. "He was my favorite. We used to—"

Dad's words were cut off by a rumbling sound. The ship began to shake.

Edgar eeeped in alarm.

What's that? I thought.

"It's the beast!" cried Dad, answering even though Snout had not spoken my words aloud. "It's still disturbed by the fight we had here with BKR and Smorkus Flinders."

"So this is just indigestion?" asked Snout as the ship shuddered again.

"When you're inside a creature this big, indigestion can be fatal!" replied my father urgently. Even as he spoke, we heard another rumble. The ship lurched sideways.

"We've got to get out of here!" cried Dad. "Right now! Flinge Iblik, contact the *Ferkel.* Tell them to follow me."

Snout went to the ship's radio. No sooner had he delivered the message than he cried, "Selima Khan! She's still outside. We can't leave her!"

Racing past Seymour and me, he plunged through the door of the ship, into the heaving belly of the beast.

CHAPTER

3

Indigestion

MY FATHER SWORE WHEN HE SAW SNOUT LEAVE.
Turning to Seymour and me, he shouted, "Go to
the door. See if you can spot Snout and Selima
Khan. I can only give them a couple of minutes.
Then we'll have to head out of here."

Edgar clung to our neck, eeeping like crazy, as
we hurried to the door of the ship.

Our friends were nowhere in sight.

We've got to find them, I thought urgently.

Got any bright ideas? asked Seymour as another spasm shook the walls.

Yeah—we go look.

You've got to be kidding! It's dangerous out there!

As if to prove Seymour's point, a huge rock fell
from the ceiling, landing about ten yards from
the ship.

That's why we've got to find them! I replied,
though I was getting more frightened myself.

Well, count me out, answered Seymour. He started to back up—taking me with him, of course.

I was furious. We couldn't just leave Snout and Selima Khan. *I said, we've got to find them!* I thought fiercely.

Then I did something that astonished both of us: I took control of our body. Leaping through the door, I landed on all sixes and raced in the direction Selima Khan had headed when she left the ship.

What are you doing? demanded Seymour. *Where are you going? This is my body. Give it back!*

"EEEEEeeeeEEEEeeeeEEEEEp!" wailed Edgar, still clinging desperately to our neck.

I didn't say anything; I was putting all my attention into looking for Snout.

I've been bodyjacked! accused Seymour.

I'll give it back as soon as we've found Snout! I replied, hoping to shut him up so I could concentrate.

Give it back now, or I'll never speak to you again!

Is that a promise?

Before Seymour could answer, the ground rippled beneath us as if a wave was rushing through it. The movement knocked us off our feet. A nearby stone column collapsed, just missing us.

Dust got in our eye. It stung, and we began blinking like crazy.

Turn back! pleaded Seymour.

Ignoring him, I scrambled to our feet and hurried forward. *Snout!* I thought desperately. *Snout, where are you?*

He didn't answer. Not surprising, since we weren't in contact at the moment.

We kept going, Seymour grumbling all the way. Then, scrambling over an undulating pile of rock, we saw them.

It was worse than I had feared. Selima Khan was trapped under a pile of rubble, buried from the waist down. Her eyes were closed, and she wasn't moving. I wondered whether she was unconscious . . . or dead.

"Help me!" cried Snout desperately when he saw us. "We've got to get her out!" He was already pawing at the rocks, flinging them away from her body as fast as he could.

Selima Khan moaned, and I felt a surge of relief. At least she was still alive.

I raced to Snout's side.

Okay, thought Seymour grudgingly. *As long as we're here, I suppose we can help.*

We started to dig, our little blue paws scrabbling at the loose stones. Seymour's body turned out to be well designed for the job—we were able to use our middle and back legs at

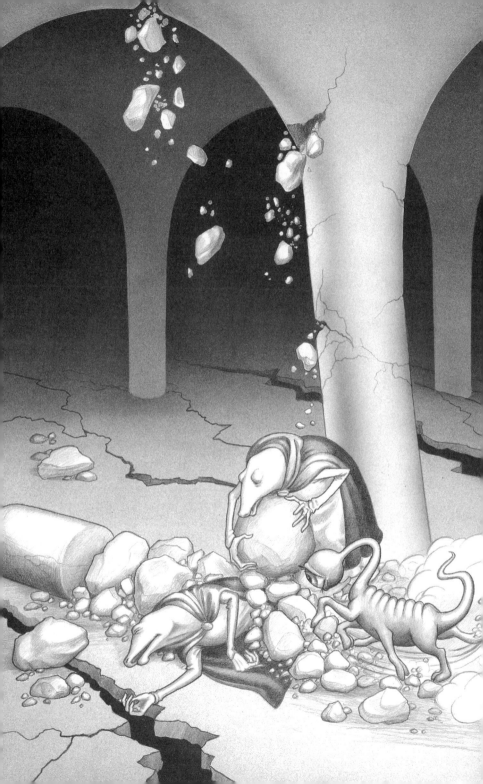

the same time, so we had four paws going instead of just two.

Suddenly I heard a horrible cracking noise above us.

Don't look up! thought Seymour, even as I did exactly that. A rain of dust and pebbles showered down, filling our huge eye with grit. I longed for a mouth so I could howl out in agony. Thick tears welled up, washing away some of the grit, but none of the pain.

Edgar, picking up on our distress, eeeped like crazy.

I told you not to look up! thought Seymour bitterly. *If you're going to steal someone's body, you should take better care of it.*

Shut up and dig! I replied, trying not to let him know how guilty I felt—which he probably did anyway, since we didn't have many secrets inside that head.

We dug.

A pillar of fire erupted next to us.

We doubled our efforts, trying to ignore our blurred vision, and the burning pain in our huge eye.

Suddenly Snout stood and closed his own eyes. At first I wondered why he had stopped helping. Then I decided he was trying to make mental contact with my father, to tell him where we were.

It must have worked, because a minute later the *Jean* came zooming into the cavern. It was only a couple of feet long now, and I realized it must have the same shrinking capacity as the *Ferkel*. At first, I figured Dad would just shrink us, too, and that would get Selima Khan free.

Are you kidding! scoffed Seymour. *If he shrinks her right now, one of these rocks will roll in and squash her flat. Come on—let's help Snout with that big one.*

We stepped beside the Mental Master and helped him push against the large boulder pinning down Selima Khan's left leg. As we worked the floor beneath us rocked and heaved, the movements so wild we could hardly stay on our feet. Sounds like thunder rumbled around us, punctuated by the hiss of gas. I was afraid the whole chamber would explode before we could get Selima Khan free. Either that, or collapse on top of us.

Suddenly the *Ferkel* flew into sight. It, too, had shrunk down. It hovered next to my father's ship.

"Work together!" shouted Snout to Seymour and me. "Don't push again until I count three."

It wasn't easy to wait, even for a few seconds, with the chaos that was raging around us. More rocks fell from the ceiling. Flames continued to erupt on all sides.

"One!" cried Snout, bellowing to be hea١. "Two! *Three!*"

We pushed with all our might.

The boulder rolled forward a few inches, then rocked back.

Selima Khan groaned in pain.

"Again!" called Snout. "One. Two! *THREE!*"

Again we pushed. Again the boulder rolled forward, then began to teeter back.

"Push!" shrieked Snout. *"PUSH!"*

We pushed, straining so hard I could feel something snap in our shoulder.

At the same moment the boulder rolled away.

Almost instantly a purple ray shot out from Dad's ship, and we began to shrink. Soon the falling rocks looked like falling mountains. By the time we were down to a couple of inches, the flames seemed as high as skyscrapers. But almost instantly another ray pulled us into the ship.

Safe at last! I thought, so relieved I could almost ignore our throbbing eye and the sharp stab of pain in our shoulder.

As if reading my mind, Dad said grimly, "Now, all we have to do is get out of here in one piece."

He was right, of course. We weren't anywhere near safe yet. Not while we were still inside the beast.

"Captain Grakker!" Dad snapped into the radio. "Follow me."

We started a desperate flight through the belly of the beast, dodging the falling rocks, the bursts of flame, the sudden contractions of the stony walls.

Snout crouched beside Selima Khan, holding her hand. His eyes were closed, and I got the feeling he was trying to beam mental energy into her, to keep her alive through the sheer force of his mind.

As for Seymour and me, our shoulder was throbbing with pain and our eyeball felt as if someone had attacked it with sandpaper. Thick tears continued to well up, making it hard for us to see. Even so, we focused our blurry vision on the large viewscreens.

By the glow of the ship's exterior lights we could see that we were hurtling through rocky tunnels, coming terrifyingly close to the walls, especially on the turns.

Suddenly the ship jolted forward, as if we had been struck from behind. It tumbled end over end, tossing us about like Ping-Pong balls in a shoebox.

"What's happening?" cried Snout.

"More indigestion," replied my father grimly, gripping the controls so tightly his knuckles turned white. "The beast is expelling some gas."

Great! I thought to Seymour. *We're caught in a giant fart storm!*

At least the ship has its own air supply, he replied—which made me wonder what the fart of a vast stone beast would smell like, anyway.

That was about all I had time to wonder. Dad had got the ship on a straight course again.

Unfortunately, that course had us racing directly toward a collision with a solid stone wall.

CHAPTER
4

Gone with the Wind

Duck! THOUGHT SEYMOUR.

We dove for the floor, where we hid our aching eye under our front paws.

To our astonishment, Dad began to laugh.

We looked up. The stone wall was opening in front of us, the hole in the center expanding the way the iris of your eye does when you go into a dark place. The ship shot through the opening with, oh, *inches* to spare.

I wanted to ask Dad if he had known that was going to happen. But Snout was focusing all his attention on Selima Khan, and couldn't or wouldn't speak for me.

Your dad probably figured the gas had to go somewhere, pointed out Seymour. *I did, too.*

Yeah, right, I replied. *Like I don't know what you're thinking.*

We were in another tunnel now, but it was

long and straight—which was just as well, since we were still moving far faster than we should have been. At least this tunnel didn't seem to be spasming.

"We have now left the beast," announced my father. "However, we are still underground."

A few miles later the tunnel curved upward. The curve grew more abrupt; soon we were traveling straight up.

"Not long now," muttered Dad.

He was right. Seconds later we shot into the open. It was early evening, and seven or eight of the planet's tiny moons were riding high in a purple sky. As Dad maneuvered the ship, I could see we had come out through something that looked like a volcanic cone. It reminded me of my science project—the one the aliens had partially eaten when I first met them.

Soon the *Ferkel* was traveling alongside us.

"Quite a ride, Ah-rit," burped Phil over the radio.

"I long to fill your lives with adventure," replied my father, sounding as if he had actually enjoyed it. "Follow me, please; I want to check on something."

It wasn't long before we could see the Mentat on our viewscreen. The home and school of the Mental Masters, the Mentat was a gigantic tree so big its base would cover six football fields.

From this trunk, which is several hundred feet high, grow dozens of wooden towers, some of them stretching up for miles.

According to Snout, the tree of the Mentat is the biggest living thing in the galaxy. It had also been our prison when we were locked away in its roots for our crime of ignoring orders from Galactic Headquarters so we could go after BKR. We had escaped with the help of Selima Khan.

My father was the founder of the Mentat. I realized now that he wanted to be sure it had survived the beast's attack of indigestion before we moved on.

It had . . . but not without damage. Cracks laced the surface of the long root-road that led from ground level to where the tree-towers began. Three of those towers had split at their base and were leaning out at crazy angles—one of them seemingly held in place only by the branch-bridge connecting it to its neighbor. Repair crews were already at work.

Dad sighed. "It will stand," he said.

We flew on, finally landing on the far side of the planet. The moment we touched down, Snout got my father to help him carry Selima Khan into the *Ferkel*, which had a much more sophisticated sick bay than the *Jean*. They placed her on one of the healing tables, then switched on the blue light. Snout sat beside her, still focusing his own energy on her as well.

Madame Pong helped Seymour and I limp up onto another of the tables. She gently washed out our aching eye, then turned on the blue light.

I had asked Madame Pong about those lights once.

"Oh, your body has tremendous healing powers," she had replied. "The blue lamps simply enhance and accelerate the natural process."

However it worked, it took only about an hour before both our eye and our shoulder were feeling completely better. Once they were all right, I thought to Seymour, *Come on. I need to get something.*

With Edgar clinging to our back, we trotted along to my room—though it wasn't going to be my room for a while now, I thought bitterly, since the *Ferkel* was going to leave us behind. Seymour didn't wear clothes, so there wasn't much in the room I actually needed. What I *wanted* was the ring Madame Pong had given me. That, and a book called *Secrets of the Mental Masters*, which had come from Snout.

The ring was right where I had left it. But Seymour's stubby blue paws were clumsy, and it was hard for us to put it on.

I wish you had fingers! I thought sharply.

And I wish I had my body all to myself! he

35

replied, equally sharply. That was enough to shut me up. Mom had always taught me to be gracious when I was a guest, and, like it or not, at the moment I was a guest in Seymour's body.

The book was even harder to deal with than the ring, since Seymour was basically a six-*legged* animal and didn't have anything that really qualified as arms. Not having a mouth, we couldn't carry it that way, either.

How do you creatures get along most of the time? I asked, breaking my vow not to criticize almost as soon as I had made it.

Most of the time, replied Seymour icily, *we chiblings manage to bond with an intelligent, fully functioning creature. It is a symbiotic relationship. We do things for them, they do things for us. Most of the time we do not have that other creature actually sharing our body with us. Most of the time that creature carries its own weight.*

That pretty effectively put me in my place. But it didn't solve the issue of the book.

Finally we went to look for Elspeth.

"Hi, Roddie," she said, when we walked through her door. "Hi, Seymour. Wasn't that a cool ride? I especially liked the part when the ship was going end over end. Did your ship do that, too? It was tons cooler than anything at Disney World."

It figured that Elspeth would like something where real death was a possibility.

"Oh, I forgot you can't talk," she said. Her voice was sweet, and I knew she hadn't forgotten at all. She just liked to grind it in. "Did you want something?"

We trotted to her door, then back to her, then back to her door again, pretty much the way my dog Bonehead does whenever he wants to go outside.

"You want me to follow you?" cried Elspeth, clapping her hands.

She knew perfectly well what we wanted. She was just having a good time pretending she was the star of some old animal movie or something. I half expected her to say, "Good girl, Lassie. Now, go get the sheriff and let him know we need help!"

Finally we got her to follow us to my room.

"Now, what could you possibly want in here?" she asked—ignoring the fact that we were practically pounding the book with our front paws.

"Goodness, what could it be?" she said, tapping her chin as if she was thinking. I was pretty sure she *was* thinking—thinking how else she could bug me. I was getting ready to take back all the nice things I had accidentally thought about her in the last month when Seymour said, *Too bad we couldn't have left her in the belly of the beast.*

Oh, she's not that bad, I replied—which annoyed me, since I didn't really want to say anything nice about Elspeth at all at the moment. I just didn't like other people bad-mouthing her. After all, she was *my* cousin. Bad-mouthing her was my job.

"The book?" she cried suddenly, as if it hadn't been obvious for the last five minutes. "Is that what you want, Roddie?"

We nodded our eye up and down.

"Well, why didn't you say so?"

I wish we had a freeze-gun, thought Seymour.

And a trigger finger, I added, having decided I didn't care *what* he said about Elspeth.

All too soon it was time for the first of our separations. Grakker and Phil stood in front of the *Ferkel* and solemnly shook hands (or paws, or leaves) with each of us.

Snout was the last to say good-bye to them. "Farewell, my captain," he whispered, embracing Grakker. To my surprise, Grakker hugged him back. "Farewell, faithful friend," he growled. "Be well until we meet again. That's an order."

As for me, I never know what to say in situations like this. So for the moment, I was actually glad that I didn't have a mouth.

Grakker and Phil climbed into the *Ferkel.* The rest of us, including Selima Khan, climbed into my father's ship. Our plan was to take Selima Khan back to the other side of Planet Mentat, where she would continue to do whatever it was she had been doing for my father—some kind of spying, from what I could make out. Then we would leave for Kryndamar, where Elspeth, Snout, Madame Pong, and Seymour and I were going to wait while Dad and Tar Gibbons went looking for BKR.

We landed in front of a cave. Selima Khan said a quiet farewell to each of us, pausing longest in front of my father, who bent his neck until their foreheads touched. They stood that way for a moment or two.

"Farewell, Ah-rit Alber Ite," murmured Selima Khan at last. "May your journey be successful."

She turned to leave the ship. As she did, Snout positioned himself beside her. She looked at him for a moment, then shrugged and nodded.

They left the ship together.

I glanced at my father.

"Flinge Iblik will be back soon enough," he said.

Indeed, it wasn't more than five minutes before Snout stepped through the ship's door. He was silent, and I was sorry to see that his long face was drooping.

"Geez," said Elspeth, "what's wrong with *you?*"

Sometimes it was useful to have her around, since she would ask the kind of questions my mother had trained me not to. It didn't do any good in this case, though. Snout merely shook his head and said, "It's a personal matter."

Dad took the controls, and we headed for Kryndamar.

One of the reasons Madame Pong had suggested Kryndamar was that it was fairly close to Planet Mentat. Personally, I would have been happier if she had chosen someplace farther away, because the trip there was going to be the last time I had with my father for a while. ("Maybe the last time *ever*," whispered a nasty voice at the back of my brain—not Seymour, this time, but my own fear speaking to me.)

Even at the speed of light, which no starships are able to reach, another star system would be years, if not centuries, away. But by jumping between dimensions, our ship was able to cross great distances in short times.

Like a day.

I didn't sleep at all during the trip. Seymour and I stayed by my father's side, asking him questions when Snout was there to interpret, just enjoying his company when he was not.

It seemed as if only hours had passed before we completed our last dimensional jump and Dad announced, "There she is, Rod. Your new temporary home. Kryndamar."

Ahead of us floated a lovely blue-and-green sphere.

"I think you will like it here," said Madame Pong, who was standing behind me. "I selected Kryndamar both because it was within easy travel distance and because it is largely uninhabited. However, it is also extraordinarily beautiful. In fact, it has been designated as one of the treasures of the galaxy—which is one reason it is largely uninhabited. No one is allowed to settle here, and while some vacations are permitted, they are highly limited. All in all, not a bad place to hide from BKR."

We landed at the edge of a beautiful lagoon. The sand of the wide beach was a delicate pink. The air (Seymour and I breathed through our skin) was as sweet as any I had ever smelled. Clear green water lapped at the shore.

The beach, which was about twenty-five yards wide, ended at a forest. Even though the air was still, the leaves rustled and moved constantly, sighing and murmuring as if their hearts were breaking. Water dripped from the tips of the leaves. I wondered why, since it wasn't raining, until Madame Pong, murmuring to herself, said, "Ah, the weeping forests of Kryndamar."

We unloaded our supplies from the ship, including some inflatable shelters, a box of clothes

Elspeth had had the ship create for her, and a portable food synthesizer.

Then it was time for Dad and Tar Gibbons to go. Those final good-byes were hard. I still couldn't believe that having finally found my father, I was going to lose him again. True, he was only going away so he could try to recover my body from our enemy. But the fact that he was going *without* me at his side made me feel as if I was going to explode with anger, sorrow, frustration, and who knows what else.

"Come on, Rod," he said. "Let's take a walk."

We wandered along the beach, Dad and Seymour and I. Edgar rode on our shoulder, cooing and chittering to himself. Snout stayed behind, so that we could be alone, which made it more private, but also meant that Dad had to do all the talking. After a while we sat and stared out at the water. I liked the sound it made as it lapped against the shore.

Dad picked up a handful of sand and let it run between his fingers. "Rod, I want you to know that I will do everything I can to get your body back. But I won't make cheap promises, and the truth is, I don't know what's going to happen. All I can promise is that I will try, and that I will not rest until we are together again."

He moved around so that he was looking into our big eye. "I wanted to be done with all this,

son—to just stay home with you and the twins and your mother. But the world doesn't always let us do what we want."

I nodded.

Dad nodded back. Then he put his arms around the silly blue body that I shared with Seymour and hugged us tight.

We walked back to the ship in silence. Night had fallen, and three huge silver moons were riding low in the black sky.

The formal farewells were made, but Dad and I had already had our real good-bye. Even so, I had one more shock when Tar Gibbons came to me and said, "My *krevlik*, when you pledged yourself to me, you vowed absolute obedience until your training was over. You have been a faithful student, and it grieves me greatly that there must be a break in that training. But that is the way things are. Because of this break, I must release you from your pledge."

No! I thought, so upset that Seymour and I reared back on our hind legs.

The Tar raised a finger. "Warrior Science tells us that to fight the tide is to drown. When we meet again, if we meet again, I will gladly accept you as my *krevlik* once more. Until then, you must be free to learn from others."

The Tar kissed me on both cheeks, then turned

and followed my father into the ship. I blinked away a tear as I watched them disappear through the door.

Our little group—Madame Pong, Snout, Elspeth, and Seymour and Edgar and I—stood on the sand and watched the *Jean* fly away.

Behind us, the trees of Kryndamar wept and moaned.

CHAPTER
5

Water Boy

THE FIRST NIGHT WE SLEPT ON THE BEACH. THE AIR was warm and sweet, and it seemed a good place to be. Using foot-long sticks, Madame Pong and Snout set a perimeter ring around us.

"What good will those do?" asked Elspeth scornfully.

"They will alert us to intruders," said Madame Pong.

Elspeth snorted. "By the time an intruder is that close, we'll be cooked meat if it wants to do something to us."

"You misunderstand," said Madame Pong. "The sensing range of the sticks extends outward from where we place them. We'll know if anything comes within a hundred yards of us. Does that make you feel better, dear?"

If I had had a mouth, I would have smiled. Elspeth likes to be called "dear" about as much

46

as I like it when she calls me "Roddie." I suspected Madame Pong knew that, too; she seemed to save the name for whenever Elspeth was being particularly obnoxious.

Elspeth had ignored what I thought was the more important question, namely, "What kind of intruders are you expecting?"

Seymour and I tapped at Snout's leg, indicating we wanted to make contact. Once the connection was open, I asked my question. Though Snout could have answered himself, he relayed the question to Madame Pong, so Elspeth could hear the answer, too.

"We're not *expecting* any, Rod," said Madame Pong. "But it's always better to be prepared. Occasionally vacationers venture here, as I mentioned. There is also the possibility of other exiles, such as ourselves, and while vacationers are not likely to be hostile, other exiles are. Then there are . . . oh, you might call them oddballs, I guess; beings who just don't fit in wherever they happen to be, and so rove the galaxy, looking for a home. Now, the chances of any of those stumbling upon us are quite small. But then, what are the chances that *we* would be here?"

"What about animals?" I asked, again via Snout.

"They should be no problem," said Madame Pong smoothly. "Unless"—and here she shuddered just slightly—"unless we should happen to be in the path of a worm migration."

"A worm migration?" asked Elspeth in astonishment.

"Imagine a billion worms all going the same place at once," said Snout solemnly.

Edgar eeeped in alarm.

"So what's the problem?" asked Elspeth, sounding a little less confident than usual. "I mean, how fast can worms move?"

"Fast enough," said Madame Pong.

"Will they eat us?" asked Elspeth, looking at the ground nervously.

Madame Pong laughed. "Of course not."

Elspeth relaxed. "Then what's the problem?" she repeated.

"Slime," said Snout. "They'll slime us." He yawned. "Good night, Elspeth. Sleep well."

He took out his sleeping pocket—a piece of fabric about the size of a man's wallet that gets a couple of hundred times bigger when you expose it to air—and gave it a shake. In a minute or two it was ready. After taking off his cape, he climbed in.

"Look at that sky," said Madame Pong quietly.

Seymour and I looked up. Beside us, I could hear Elspeth gasp.

The sky was extraordinarily clear, and a fourth moon had just slipped above the horizon. Turning our eye to the right, we saw a vast curtain of rose-colored light rippling against the blackness.

Madame Pong smiled. "It's nice to visit other worlds, isn't it? Well, I'll see you kids in the morning."

She shook out her sleeping pocket. As it was expanding she unfastened her blue cape and draped it over the pocket like an extra blanket. "Such lovely air," she murmured as she climbed inside. "Don't stay up too late, children."

Elspeth sat on the sand, looking around nervously. "Roddie," she said after a few minutes, "are you scared?"

What could I say?

I mean, I didn't have a mouth.

Seymour and I trotted over to stand next to her.

"Blink once if you're scared, twice if you're not scared," said Elspeth.

Are we scared? asked Seymour.

I'm scared we'll be stuck like this forever, I said.

That's good enough, replied Seymour. *Let's blink once.*

We did so, then went back to our sleeping pocket, which Madame Pong had already shaken out for us. We could have climbed inside, but Seymour was not designed to wear clothes, and his body did fine out in the open. So we just curled up on top of the pocket, which was comfy and snuggy, and closed our eye. Edgar scrambled over our side, tucked his furry little body next to our middle, and began eeeping drowsily.

As we were drifting off, lulled by the murmur of the waves and the weeping of the trees, Snout sent us a message: *Odds of a worm migration coming this way—about a billion to one. Odds of Elspeth improving her behavior without help—about the same. Sleep well, young friends.*

Seymour and I curled our long neck so that our big eye was resting against our front paws. Edgar gave one last groggy eeep. Then we all fell asleep.

I don't know how many hours later it was when we were woken by the beeping of the perimeter alarm. Seymour and I leaped to our feet. But it was nothing serious. A purple bird, or something like a bird, was stalking down the beach—looking for breakfast, from the way it was staring into the water as it walked.

Well, if the early bird really does catch the worm, it should relieve Elspeth, I thought.

A pearly gray light was blossoming over the lagoon.

Seymour and I stretched luxuriously, enjoying the feel of the sand beneath our paws. A lot of people don't like to get up that early, but my grandfather is a farmer, and my mother still keeps the kind of hours she learned as a kid. So in our house it's always been "early to rise"—which is okay with me. The quiet, peaceful hours of early dawn are just about my favorite time of day.

The others were up, too, of course. Well, all except Elspeth. Despite the alarm, she was lying facedown in her sleeping pocket, snoring gently. I wondered what time she had gotten to sleep.

Despite all the bad stuff that was going on, at the moment I was excited, almost happy. Planet Mentat was the first alien world that I had visited (at least, in our dimension). But we had been imprisoned soon after landing, and almost my entire experience there had been underground. Here on Kryndamar it was different. At last I felt like I had achieved my lifelong dream of visiting another planet.

"Good morning, RodandSeymour," said Madame Pong, mushing our names into one word. "Did you sleep well?"

We nodded our eye at her.

"Good." She rummaged around in one of the supply containers until she found a small device called a winder-binder (because it winds and binds). She tucked one end of her sleeping pocket into the thing, which began compressing the pocket to its original size. As she worked, she said, "We should all bathe this morning. I know your culture is much more sensitive about nudity than most, so we will go separately. Since you two don't have clothes anyway, perhaps you would like to go first?"

Depends on how warm the water is, thought Seymour. I caught an edge of nervousness in his tone.

Snout, who had opened a connection to us, spoke the words aloud.

Madame Pong smiled. "I think you'll find it to your liking."

Let's go in, I urged Seymour.

But I can't swim!

This surprised me. Live in someone's head, and you still don't know everything about them. Of course, the issue had never come up before.

Don't worry, I replied. *I'm a great swimmer. Besides, we don't have to go in over our eye or anything.*

Okay, Uncle Rod, he thought uneasily. *If you insist.*

We sent our decision to Snout.

"They'll go first," he said aloud.

Seymour, Edgar, and I trotted down to the water. The first wave that rolled in got Edgar's fur wet. Eeping in alarm, the little furball scrambled back up the beach and onto our sleeping pocket.

Ready? I asked.

Ready as I'll ever be, replied Seymour, not sounding all that happy.

We waded in. The water was warm, and perfectly clear. Through it we could see brightly colored creatures scuttling around in the sand. They seemed neither alarmed, nor interested in our presence. A little farther out we saw some fish-like things, and also something long and flat—almost like a thick piece of paper—that moved through the water by undulating its orange body.

A wave knocked us off our feet, and I found the first flaw in my plan about swimming. Since Seymour and I breathed through our skin, once we were underwater, we started to suffocate.

Seymour panicked at once, and his panic affected me. We burst through to the surface, scrambling for a foothold, trying desperately to get the larger part of our body into the air. We could hear Edgar eeeping with alarm up on shore.

Another wave knocked us under.

Air. We needed *air!*

Stay calm, I thought, trying to keep my attention focused. But Seymour's panic was like an eggbeater, scrambling my thoughts.

Our panic doubled when we felt the current pulling us away from the shore, into the lagoon.

"I'm coming!" cried Snout, splashing into the water. "Hold on! *Hold on!*"

He dove forward and grabbed at one of our legs. He caught it for an instant, but it was slick with water and slipped out of his hand.

Thrashing wildly, dizzy with lack of air, Seymour and I were swept away from the shore.

CHAPTER
6

The Weeping Forest

THE PEACEFUL WATER OF THE LAGOON NOW SEEMED like a deadly trap. Unable to breathe, my reactions scrambled by Seymour's panic, all I could think was that we were going to die.

Sorry, Seymour, I thought as the blackness closed over us. *I shouldn't have—*

Suddenly we ran into something. A moment later we were lifted from the water. Air, glorious air, caressed our skin, and we were able to breathe once more.

I looked down, wondering how Snout had managed to catch us. To my astonishment, we were being held up by a man-shaped creature. He was nearly a head taller than Grakker, but just as muscular. Under his blue-green arms, stretching from his elbows to his sides, was a spiky membrane—sort of like the fin that rises from a fish's back. He was hairless, naked, and cranky.

"Can't a being rest in peace *anywhere* in this galaxy?" he roared. For a moment I thought he was going to fling us back into the water. Instead, muttering and cursing beneath his breath, he tucked us under his arm and waded toward shore. The spikes from his fin-thing were poking our skin. We didn't complain. (Not that we could have said anything if we had wanted to.)

Snout was still in the water. He looked exhausted and bedraggled, and I could tell he had continued trying to catch us, even after it was obviously hopeless. Getting to his feet, he waded to shore beside us.

Madame Pong was standing at the water's edge. "A thousand thanks," she said, putting her long, yellow fingers together and making a tiny bow.

Ignoring her thanks, our rescuer dumped Seymour and me onto the pink sand. "What are you doing here, anyway?" he growled. "This planet is restricted!"

"I might ask the same of you," said Madame Pong quietly. "However, as you have done us a great favor, I will answer your question. We have come here for a brief rest." Without missing a beat she gestured toward Seymour and me and said, "Our pet here is not used to the water, and made an error . . . an error that would have been fatal without your intervention. Again, our thanks."

Pet? thought Seymour in outrage.

It's a good disguise, I replied—though I was fairly annoyed by the term myself.

"I also came here to get away," said the water-man. "Didn't count on having to rescue some land crawler from his own stupidity." He narrowed his eyes. "You going to be here long?"

"We're leaving this area later this morning," replied Madame Pong, sidestepping the larger question of how long we were going to be on the planet.

"Name's Quat," said the blue-green man, sticking out his hand. He had webbing between his fingers.

"I am Madame Pong," replied our diplomat, taking his hand without a second thought. "This is my colleague, Flinge Iblik. And this," she said, gesturing toward my cousin, "is Elspeth."

"Weird-looking creature," said Quat.

"The galaxy is vast and strange," said Madame Pong with a shrug. "Again, our profound thanks for bringing our pet back to us. Perhaps you would care to share a meal?"

"Maybe some other time," said Quat, sounding surprised. He began backing into the water. "Enjoy your vacation," he said grudgingly. "Glad to have been of service. Also be glad to see you go."

By this time he was up to his knees. Suddenly he dropped backward.

To my astonishment, he disappeared so completely I couldn't see a trace of him, even with Seymour's superior vision.

"Remarkably effective camouflage technique," murmured Madame Pong.

"So what was he?" asked Elspeth, after waiting a few minutes to be sure he was gone. "Vacationer, exile, or oddball?"

"He may well have been all three," said Snout. "Let's just be glad he was here."

"Yes. Unusually lucky, wasn't it," murmured Madame Pong.

I couldn't be sure, but I thought she sounded suspicious.

That afternoon we went into the forest. The weeping of the trees, which had been a pleasant, if melancholy, background sound on the beach, was nearly overwhelming here. The sound—and the drops that fell slowly and steadily from their leaves—seemed to bring up all my own sorrows, pulling my losses from the back of my mind to the front. Without intending to, I found myself weeping as well—huge, thick tears that rolled out of our enormous eye and plopped to the ground. Seymour didn't caution me against crying this time because he was crying, too—though whether in sympathy, or for sorrows of his own, I wasn't sure.

We're not going to stay in these trees, are we?
I asked Snout.

His own sorrow pulsed beneath his answer: *No.
Not all the groves of Kryndamar are filled with
weeping trees. We'll go elsewhere.*

He stifled a sob and walked on.

A little deeper into the wood we came to a
place where the trees were weeping and moaning
far more loudly than before. Their branches
moved with their sorrow, occasionally flailing
wildly, as if tearing at themselves.

Beneath one of the trees I noticed a pile of
white sticks. At least, I thought they were white
sticks. A closer look showed me that they were
bones.

That struck me as being the saddest thing I
had ever seen.

The trees, weeping and moaning, made that
sorrow even worse, so thick it almost choked me.

Their sorrow seemed to be gripping all of us.
Our entire group stopped. Heartstricken, we listened to the trees. Then we all sat down and
began to weep, too, sobbing as if our hearts
were breaking.

Every sorrow I had ever experienced seemed to
rush in on me. Little griefs and large ones tumbled over each other, the memory of a lost toy
coming side by side with television images of
starving children that had made it impossible for

me to sleep the night I saw them. Under them all pulsed my need for my father, my fear that I would never see him again, and my desperate longing to have my own body back.

Seymour and I wept in silence, of course. Not so the others.

Pressing her face to the ground, Elspeth sobbed, "Like me. Like me. Please, won't *somebody* like me?"

At the same time Madame Pong threw back her head and let out a weird wail, a piercing ululation that seemed to come from the depths of some great blackness; the sound sent a shiver along the spine I shared with Seymour.

Snout howled and moaned, rocking from side to side. Among his cries of sorrow sometimes I heard the words "Selima Khan" and "Grakker."

Even Edgar's eeeping seemed to be tinged with tragedy.

I was having a flashback to *The Wizard of Oz* (when I was little I used to cry because Dorothy couldn't get back home) when I realized what was going on. It was a memory of the Wicked Witch of the West crooning: "Poppies! Poppies will make them sleep" that did it.

Poppies will make them sleep, Trees will make them weep, I thought miserably.

And that was when it hit me. We were being trapped by the trees! Was it possible we might

59

be stuck in this place forever—might die here, weeping with the melancholy trees?

Don't think that! wailed Seymour. *It's too sad!*

Come on! I replied. *We've got to get out of here!*

I can't get up, he thought dismally. *I'm too unhappy.*

Again, as I had in the belly of the beast, I took control of our legs—which made Seymour even sadder. *You've stolen my body,* he mourned. *I have no life!*

You certainly won't have a life if we don't get away from these trees, I replied fiercely.

Even so, step one was accomplished. We were on our feet.

But now what? With no mouth, I couldn't yell a warning to the others. And my little paws weren't strong enough to drag them out of the clearing.

The hopelessness of it made me want to sit down and weep.

Only one thing stopped me. I knew that if I did, I would never get up again.

CHAPTER
7

Nuts

"Action is the great cure for despair," Tar Gibbons once told me. (Actually, the Tar was always telling me stuff like that.)

The problem was, I couldn't think of what action to take—which only added to my despair. And the constant weeping of the trees kept pulling me back toward a sorrow so deep that no action seemed possible.

Seymour, retaking control of our shared body, flung us to the ground, where we shook with his sorrow. I nearly gave up, nearly joined him in his despair. But it had made me mad when he took over the body, and that anger was stronger than the sorrow.

Get up! I raged at him. *Get up!*

Tears were gushing from our eye so fast the loss of fluid was making us weak. But I got him moving again. As we scrambled to our feet, we felt something hard and round underneath us.

Nuts! Nuts from the weeping trees.

Oh, that's so sad, thought Seymour mournfully. *They've lost their nuts.*

Shut up and help! I replied. I seized control of the body again. Our little blue paws were small, but not so small I couldn't pick up a nut and fling it.

I nailed Snout right between the eyes.

He blinked and looked around. Suddenly a look of horror crossed his face, and I knew I had snapped him out of the spell.

As he leaped to his feet, I flung a nut at Elspeth. I missed, so I threw another. Bingo! Like Snout, she blinked. Unlike Snout, she went right back to her crying.

Snout himself was still looking kind of foggy, so I hurled another nut at him, too. It caught him right on the top of the head. He shook himself. Then he clamped his hands over the sides of his head and rushed from the clearing.

The fact that he had abandoned us only made me madder—which made it easier to resist the weeping of the trees.

I whacked Elspeth with another nut. "Will you stop that!" she cried, wiping the tears from her eyes with a clenched fist.

At that point Snout came running back.

"Come with me, Elspeth," he said, dragging her to her feet. "We have to get out of here."

"Let go of me!" she shouted, struggling in his grasp. "I gotta clobber Roddie!"

Well, anger had certainly broken the spell for her.

"If you stay here, all you're going to do is sit back down and cry," said Snout desperately.

Elspeth blinked, and I could tell she knew he was right.

As they ran from the clearing, I winged a nut at Madame Pong. I had saved her until last because I had a hard time hitting a lady, especially one as kind and dignified as Madame Pong.

When the nut bounced off her head, she opened her eyes and stared at me in surprise. "Oh, Rod," she wailed, her lower lip quivering. "How *could* you?"

Then she began to cry harder than ever.

That made me feel terrible, of course—so bad I almost gave in to the sorrow myself once more. But then Snout returned again, and the surge of hope I felt seemed to drive the despair away. Snout tried to pull Madame Pong to her feet. When that didn't work, he hooked his hands under her arms and dragged her, blubbering, away from the trees.

Seymour and I went trotting after him, Seymour weeping and wailing (inside our head, of course) all the way.

It was only after we were a good distance from the clearing that I realized we had forgotten Edgar.

I turned and headed back.

No! thought Seymour in alarm. *We can't go back there. We'll die!*

We have to get Edgar! I replied fiercely.

This sent him into a new tizzy of despair, which only got worse as we moved back within range of the trees. *Oh, we're scum!* he thought. *Scum! How could we have forgotten poor little Edgar! Oh, the poor fluffy baby!*

It was only the fact that his going on like this was so annoying that kept me from giving in to the trees myself. When we found Edgar, I nearly did anyway. The poor little guy was stretched out on the forest floor, eeeping in a tiny voice that sounded even sadder than the trees. If he could have talked, I was sure he would have been saying, "Abandoned! Left to die! No one loves me! No one cares!"

I knelt and nudged him.

"Eeep?" he asked in a thin, mournful tone. *"Eeeep!"*

Then he climbed onto our back.

We stood and trotted away, leaving the trees weeping and moaning behind us.

I noticed Snout go back one more time, and wondered what he was doing, since we were all out safely.

Seymour and I waited for him to come back, just in case. When he returned, he was actually smiling.

What were you doing? I asked when he opened the line of contact.

I wanted to get some of those nuts you bonked me with, he replied. *They may be interesting.*

"Well," said Madame Pong when we had settled down, dried our tears, caught our breath. "It appears we owe you our lives, Rod."

I would have said, "Aw, shucks," if I had been able to talk. I would have smiled, if I had had lips. As it was, Seymour and I just ducked our eyeball modestly.

"I, especially, am grateful," said Snout. "A Mental Master should never have succumbed to something like that."

"So why did you?" asked Elspeth, never one to let someone off the hook easily.

Snout closed his eyes. "I am not fully in balance yet. As you know, I nearly left this life when we were in Dimension X. This was not a tragedy from my point of view. I was moving on to something new, something beautiful. But Rod's father called me back, and that forced return has left me burdened with a sorrow unlike any I have ever known. Well, unlike any save one that I carry from long ago. But this new grief is so deep and so fresh that the trees were able to pull it to the surface before I realized what was happening. Thus, I was as lost as the rest of you."

He turned away. No one spoke for a moment.

It was Elspeth who finally broke the silence. "What was that thing with the trees all about, anyway?" she asked.

"I am not entirely sure," said Madame Pong. "My theory is that they were trying to entrap us so they could use us as food."

"*Food?*" yelped Elspeth.

Madame Pong shrugged. "It would be a long-term process. Trapped by despair, unable to move, we would die. Over the years our bodies would rot. In doing so, they would enrich the soil. Then the trees' roots would take in the added nutrition."

"So they were trying to kill us?" asked Elspeth with a shudder.

"I doubt it was conscious," said Madame Pong. "It may be a tactic evolved over millions of years. I have a vague recollection of some legend about the weeping trees. I'll look it up, when I have a chance."

"Did you know they would do this when you brought us here?" demanded Elspeth.

She took the words right out of my mouth, so to speak.

"Goodness, no!" said Madame Pong. "I would never knowingly bring you into danger. Most of the trees are merely mildly melancholy, as you heard at the beach. I suspect these are a wilder, older species, not well known. Now come on, we need to get moving. I want to find a place to make our permanent camp before it gets dark."

It took several hours, but finally we found a spot on the bank of a small pond that we all agreed was just fine. A clear stream ran into the pond, and Snout tested the water with some kit he had, to make sure it was safe to drink. The trees were quiet (that was a relief!) and not too thick. The ground was littered with twigs and leaves that Madame Pong said would work well in our synthesizer. And there was enough level space to put up our shelters.

We had two of these shelters—one for Madame Pong and Elspeth, one for Snout, Edgar, and Seymour and me.

Elspeth promptly dubbed them "the Boys' Room" and "the Girls' Room." That wasn't quite accurate, since we put up another small shelter about twenty feet away, after Snout used a blaster to open a good-sized pit in the ground, and this was both the boys' room *and* the girls' room, at least in the way those terms are usually used.

All in all, it was a little like taking a camping trip—though our shelters were a heck of a lot nicer than any tent I had ever been in. For one thing, their walls were temperature regulating; no matter how hot or cold it got outside, the inside was always perfectly comfortable. For another thing, the floor of the shelters was made of the same material as the sleeping pockets, and walking on it was like walking on the deepest, thickest carpet you ever imagined.

That night we made a campfire. Then we all sat around it while Madame Pong told hilarious stories about the snavel and the wonkus, two characters they liked to talk about on her home planet.

Afterward, Snout told the scariest ghost story I had ever heard.

Do you believe in ghosts? I asked him, after he was done.

Existence comes in many forms, he replied with a shrug. *I was nearly something resembling a ghost myself, before your father called me back to this life—though it would have been quite different than the way you think of ghosts.*

What do you mean?

I was joining with other Mental Masters who have left this plane of existence. I was losing myself, becoming part of something bigger, something that— He broke off the thought, then added, *At least, I was until I was forced to come back.*

He closed his mind to me then, but not before I got a sense of loss so bitter it was as if my brain was being washed in lemon juice.

No one spoke for a while. Seymour and I stared into the fire, listening to the night sounds that drifted around us. We heard something singing softly in the trees. A bird? I wondered. An insect? Maybe something I had never even imagined? My mind was wandering off on this tangent when I realized someone was touching us on the shoulder.

"Take a walk with me," said Madame Pong, when Seymour and I looked around to see who it was.

We scrambled to our feet. Following Madame Pong, we meandered along the stream for a way. Occasionally Seymour and I would wade into the water, which seemed to chuckle, as if rebuking the trees for being so sad. Madame Pong mostly looked at the stars. The rosy curtain of light was not out this night.

When we were a fair distance from the camp, Madame Pong said, "I notice you are wearing the ring I gave you after our first adventure, Rod."

She paused, as if waiting for me to answer. After a moment of silence she went on as if I had. "It's good that you brought it. Should things go terribly wrong, the ring may prove useful."

How? I thought.

Though I couldn't speak the word out loud, Madame Pong answered anyway. Taking a deep breath, she knelt beside Seymour and me and looked directly into our big eye.

"That is a diplomat's ring," she said softly, "and it has more than one use. The important one to know about now is that if you are captured by BKR, the ring will allow you to end your life quickly and painlessly, before he can pry the fatal information from your brain."

CHAPTER
8

Mental Exercises

GEEZ, LOUISE, THOUGHT SEYMOUR. *IF I'D KNOWN what kind of messes you were going to get me into, I'd have thought twice before I let you share my brain, Uncle Rod.*

I didn't bother to answer him. And I didn't bother to point out to Madame Pong that I'm just a kid. Once I had accepted membership in the Galactic Patrol, being a kid didn't count for much when it came to excuses. But I did understand, in a deeper way than ever before, how serious this really was.

Even so, I wondered why she had left the ring with me to begin with. I mean, what if I had killed myself with it by accident? But as she explained how to use it, I soon realized that that wouldn't have been possible. The ring couldn't do its number on you until it had been activated, something that only she could do. That was sort of comforting.

It would have been even more comforting if she hadn't chosen that moment to activate it.

"Now it will be ready if you need it," she said as she slipped it back onto our paw. "The ring has other uses, of course. For one thing, it is recognized by diplomats across the galaxy. They are required to help you if you show it to them."

Well, that's a relief, thought Seymour.

When she was done with her instructions, she put her hand on top of our eye and said softly, "You are a worthy comrade, Deputy Allbright, and I am proud to share both danger and duty with you."

Her hand was empty. Even so, I felt as if I had just been knighted.

We walked back to the camp in silence. Before we went to sleep, I slipped the ring off our paw and stowed it carefully with my things. It made me nervous. Besides, we didn't have to worry about BKR at the moment.

Thanks, said Seymour as we were settling in to sleep. *I was hoping we wouldn't have to wear that all the time now.*

The next morning it was Snout's turn to invite me for a walk.

Geez, we sure are popular these days, thought Seymour as we started out after the Mental Master. We took pretty much the same path we had with Madame Pong the night before, following the stream that fed into the pond. But this time we went even farther. As we walked on, we could hear trees weeping in the distance—just normal weeping, not the fatal kind.

We are going to be here for an undetermined amount of time, thought Snout, speaking directly into my head. *It could be a few weeks; it could be many years.*

Yike! thought Seymour. I had to agree. I hadn't really thought about how long this might take.

Yike, indeed, replied Snout. *The thing is, it is not good to be idle for that amount of time. We need something worthwhile to do. Therefore, I was wondering if you would like to train with me. Not too intensely,* he added, holding up one of his long-fingered purple hands. *After all, you are not an official apprentice. And you remain Tar Gibbons's* krevlik, *even though he has released you for the time being. But there are things I can teach you that may help you on your road.*

I would be honored, I replied.

Good. We start tomorrow.

To my surprise, we started with exercises. *Physical* ones . . . like push-ups, which are utterly different when you do them in a body with six stumpy legs.

74

I thought we were going to be doing mental work, I complained.

The mind and the body are intimately connected, replied Snout, who was standing on one finger.

Are you kidding? I thought bitterly. *My body and mind are umpty squintillion miles apart.*

You are a special case, replied Snout. *Even so, the mind you are sharing with Seymour will work better if the body that carries it is in proper condition.*

If that's so, then how come the Head Council of the Mentat has given up on bodies altogether? asked Seymour.

Snout slowly returned himself to a standing position. I was impressed; he was stronger than I would have guessed. He gestured for us to try standing on one leg. At the same time, speaking aloud, he said, "In my opinion, the Head Council has forgotten the importance of balance. That is one reason I left the Mentat and joined the Galactic Patrol. Not that the patrol is perfect," he added as he grabbed our legs to keep us from falling.

After about an hour of exercising, Seymour and I were exhausted. Snout, however, showed no signs of wear and tear at all.

I wouldn't be so tired if I was in my own body, I told Seymour. *I exercised a lot when I was training with Tar Gibbons.*

Oh, shut up, he replied.

Under the circumstances, he was probably justified.

That night we began another aspect of our training. After dinner Snout took us to the top of a hill he had found while Seymour and I were resting that afternoon. Sitting together, we looked out at the stars for a while, and listened to the distant weeping of the trees.

After about fifteen minutes Snout put his hand on our shoulder and asked, *What is your code, Rod?*

Huh? I replied, none too brilliantly. I thought he was asking about some kind of secret communication system.

What is your code? he repeated. *What rules do you live by? What do you believe? What will you fight for? What do you honor above all else? These are some of the things I mean when I say, "What is your code?" No being can be a Mental Master, or even a master of its own life, unless it has a code. So what is your code, Rod Allbright?*

I couldn't answer him, then. I mean, I had some vague ideas, but I had never really thought them through. I felt strange, not being able to answer. I felt that I should have thought of these things before.

We went to the hilltop every night.

Every night Snout asked me the same question.

What's your *code?* I asked, more than once.

Most of the time he just shook his head and said, "My code is not the point. It is something that grew from my heart, just as yours must grow from your own heart. Listen to your heart, Rod. It will tell what is important. It will tell you what really counts."

Yet despite that, he did give me one hint. We were lying on our backs, staring up at the stars one night, when he said out of nowhere, "I will tell you one piece of my code. I try, in all things, to act out of love, not fear. I do not always succeed, of course. If I did, I would be *the* Mental Master. But it is a useful guideline." He chuckled softly and added, "I know it is useful, because I have found that whenever I forget it, I get myself in trouble."

Every night I struggled with Snout's question. And finally I did find my answer. Not in a blinding moment of insight. It came slowly, piece by piece.

But once I had it, I knew the struggle had been worth it.

So what was it?

Sorry, but that's one thing I'm not going to tell you—and I really have told you just about everything else. But your code has got to come from your own heart, or it won't be yours at all.

The other thing that happened at night was that we sat around the campfire and told stories. Well, mostly Madame Pong and Snout told stories. Elspeth told a couple. Seymour and I, obviously, were in no condition to do any storytelling at all.

I got a kick out of the stories we heard from Madame Pong and Snout; they ranged from truly weird alien fairy tales to wild stories of their adventures with the Galactic Patrol.

One night Snout got out the nuts he had gathered from the grove of trees where we had nearly died from weeping.

"Who wants to try one?" he asked.

None of us answered. With a shrug he held one up so that we could see it in the firelight. It was beautiful, a burnished brown color with a smooth, oval shell.

He put it on a rock, picked up another rock, and cracked it open.

The odor it released was tantalizing.

Using his long fingers, he pried a piece of the meat out of the shell. Then he went into the Boys' Room. When he came back out he was carrying a small box-shaped device that had several dials and meters on it. He dropped the nut in and pushed a button. The device whirred and clicked, then dinged.

Snout studied the dials. "Well, it should be safe to eat," he said at last.

Taking another piece of nutmeat from the shell, he popped it into his mouth, and began to chew.

An instant later he burst into tears.

It was fifteen minutes before he could stop.

"These would probably be useful in therapy," he said, wiping his eyes. Then he put them back in the cloth bag where he had stored them, and returned them to our shelter.

Two nights later Quat the waterman showed up at our fireside. He was carrying a slimy-looking bag and wanted to know if we would mind his company.

"Not at all," said Madame Pong. "Please, join us."

"I brought some food to share," said Quat, reaching into his bag. A moment later he pulled out a warty thing that looked like a purple pickle.

"Here," he said, handing it to Elspeth.

She wrinkled her nose in disgust. "You expect me to eat this thing?"

"Certainly," replied Quat, reaching into the bag for another. "They're delicious."

Figures. Alien guy comes with a special treat,

and what is it? Some scrumptious food that I can't eat, because I don't have a mouth!

Don't be bitter, Uncle Rod, thought Seymour. *At least you* used *to have a mouth. I never*—

His thought was interrupted by Elspeth's scream.

CHAPTER
9

Negatrons

ELSPETH WAS STANDING ON HER FEET. "IT MOVED!" she cried. She was pointing at the warty purple thing, which was now lying on the ground in front of her. "It moved. Right in my hand. It moved!"

As if to prove the point, the purple thing doubled over, then straightened out, which caused it to bounce at least two feet into the air.

"Aaaah!" cried Elspeth, backing away from it. "Aaaaah!"

Quat began to laugh. "I forgot to tell you; you have to kill it before you can eat it!"

"I'm a vegetarian!" cried Elspeth. This was a total lie, of course. But under the circumstances, I couldn't blame her.

"But this *is* a vegetable," said Quat. "It's hard to get them this fresh. They're considered a great delicacy."

"Vegetables don't bounce," said Elspeth, who was now standing about ten feet from the campfire.

"These do," said Quat.

"If they bounce, they're animals," insisted Elspeth.

"Vegetables," replied Quat firmly. With that he took the knife from his side and skewered the purple thing he was holding. I half expected it to scream. Or bleed. Or both.

It did neither.

Quat twisted the knife and deftly sliced the thing in half. "See," he said, holding out the two parts.

The inside section, smooth and moist, looked pretty much like a purple potato.

He took a bite and smiled. "Delicious," he said, holding the other half out toward Elspeth.

She looked at Madame Pong, who responded with just the slightest nod. Elspeth swallowed and walked forward. I wondered what that was all about. Had Madame Pong been working with Elspeth while Snout was working with me? I kind of liked the thought of someone trying to turn Elspeth into a diplomat. It was sort of like training a gorilla to be a butler.

As Elspeth took the purple thing from Quat's hand, the waterguy said, "I offered it to you first because in our culture the youngest female in a group is always given great honor."

You could tell Elspeth liked that idea. She lifted the purple thing to her lips and took a bite. "Man, that's great!" she said. Then she crammed most of the rest of it into her mouth.

Madame Pong sighed.

Quat stayed for another couple of hours, though every twenty minutes or so he would go down and take a dip in the pond to get himself wet again. He even told a story or two himself— including a long one that turned out to be an underwater version of "Cinderella."

After he had left, Madame Pong said, "With luck, perhaps this experience will also be a story someday. I don't mean just our visit with Quat. I mean our entire stay on Kryndamar. A story with a happy ending."

We can call it "Madame Pong and the Exiles," I thought.

Snout spoke the words out loud for me.

"Sounds like a rock group," said Elspeth. She jumped to her feet and started playing air guitar.

"Earthlings truly are a strange people," said Snout, folding his spindly fingers over his long face.

When Snout and I began our exercises the next day he asked, *Have you noticed anything about our ability to speak to each other mentally?*

Only that we can do it, I replied. *A good thing,*

too, or I wouldn't have anyone to talk to but Seymour.

Something wrong with talking to me? asked Seymour huffily.

Think about it a little more, Rod, persisted Snout.

Suddenly I realized he was talking about the thing that had been bothering me all along. *You can contact me, but I can't contact you. So the only way I can talk to you is if you contact me first. Frankly, it's pretty annoying.*

Then I think it's time we worked on it.

This was good news. I had been wildly frustrated at having to wait for Snout to contact me before we could have a discussion.

I am now going to break our connection, thought Snout. *Let's see if you can reestablish it.*

I couldn't. I stood there, looking right at him and thinking, *Snout. Oh, Snout. Can you hear me, Snout?*

I got no response at all.

Come in, Snout. This is Rod calling. I want to talk to you.

I might as well have been thinking at a wall.

SNOUT! I thought, and suddenly the connection did open. Unfortunately, it was because Snout had opened it, not because I had gotten through to him.

We're going to try again in a second, he

thought. *This time I want you to close your eye and try to see me in your mind. See me getting your message.*

Then he broke the connection again.

I did as he asked, concentrating so hard that our body started to shake. I imagined him getting the message. I pictured his eyes going wide in astonishment at how clearly it came through. I visualized him jumping in shock and falling over at the strength of our sending.

Still no connection.

We went on that way for another hour.

Don't be frustrated, Rod, said Snout at last. *Mindspeak is an advanced technique. Most people can't even* receive *a connection without a lot of training, much less open one. So you're already ahead of the game. It's only because you have so much more need of the ability than most that I'm trying to move you forward faster than normal. I had hoped that the fact that we are so tightly connected—I'm sure it's because of that interrupted training transfer we experienced back when I first met you—would make it possible for you to reach me. We'll keep trying.*

And try we did. Every day. But no matter how hard I concentrated, I wasn't able to get through to him.

Fortunately, I was making progress with some

of Snout's other lessons: How to remember things better. How to control fear. How to control my sense of time.

But I still couldn't make that contact with Snout.

Perhaps you are generating negatrons, suggested Snout one afternoon.

Negatrons? Seymour and I asked simultaneously.

They are a powerful force created by negative thinking. The flow of negatrons has a subtle but deeply destructive effect on everything around it. Very destructive. One of the first things you have to learn as a Mental Master is how to keep from generating negatrons, and how to prevent other people's negatrons from affecting your work and well-being. They weaken the mind terribly.

Seymour and I put our front paws to our head. *Sorry!* we thought. *We didn't mean to!*

Oh, almost everyone does it sometimes, said Snout. *I heard once that BKR was working on a way to channel them into a weapon.*

To blow things up? I asked.

No, to tear them down. That's how negatrons work. It's like erosion. They slowly chip away at things. If BKR could find a way to focus them, he might be able to beam them at something good—like a family, for example—and destroy it in a matter of days. It's exactly the kind of thing he likes to do. Now, let's try again. And think positive this time!

I'm positive this is all a lot of hooey! put in Seymour.

Quiet! I replied. *You're generating negatrons.*

Well, pardon me for speaking up inside my own brain. Do you want me to go for a walk while you two play?

Will you just shut up? I thought desperately. *I'm trying to contact Snout.*

But it was no good. I still couldn't get through to him.

"I want to try something different," said Snout, the next afternoon, speaking out loud. "It may be that our physical closeness is interfering somehow. I want you to walk over that way until you can't see me anymore. Then we'll give it another try. Remember, no negative thoughts!"

Yeah, yeah, yeah, thought Seymour.

Leaving Edgar sitting on a rock in the sunshine, we trotted off in the direction Snout had indicated. It took a while before we were out of sight—partly because Seymour's eyesight was so good that we had to go much farther away than we would have if I were in my old body. Finally we went over the top of a small, tree-covered hill that blocked Snout from our view.

Again, I tried to contact him. But even concentrating with all my might, I couldn't do it. After fifteen or twenty minutes we decided to give up and head back.

Except when we did, we must have taken a wrong turn somewhere, because we couldn't find him.

Now look what you've done, Uncle Rod, thought Seymour. *We're lost!*

We are not, I replied.

But I was wrong. Not only could we not find Snout, we couldn't even find our way back to where we had been standing while we tried to contact him. We began trotting back and forth, looking for any familiar landmark. Soon we were running.

Panic seized us. We ran until our skin burned with the effort of breathing, looking for any sign of Snout, or any clue to the location of our camp.

Finally we had to face the terrible truth.

We were lost on an alien planet.

And we didn't even have a mouth to yell for help.

CHAPTER
10

Pet, Peeved

SICK WITH FEAR, SEYMOUR AND I WANDERED AROUND for at least an hour trying to find our way back to the camp.

No place we went looked familiar, and we were getting more terrified by the moment. Everything Snout had taught me about staying calm seemed to have flown out of my head.

I can't tell you what a relief it was when we stumbled into a clearing and discovered a group of beings having a picnic. There were three of them, two adults and a female child. They were pretty much standard size, with large, intelligent-looking yellow eyes and high foreheads. They had lavender skin, flowing silver hair, and noses like bananas.

But hey, who was I to think that someone else looked weird?

They were laughing and having a good time, and you could tell they really liked each other.

We watched for a while from behind a tree. Finally Seymour thought, *What do you think, Uncle Rod—shall we go over and see if they can help us?*

I don't know. . . . I replied, still nervous about exposing ourselves.

You got a better idea? asked Seymour impatiently.

At the moment I didn't have any ideas at all. So we trotted over on our little blue feet, hoping the picnickers were as friendly as they looked, and that maybe we could figure out a way to communicate with them.

"Look, Mommy," said the girl, jumping up and wrapping her arm around our neck. "It's a weird little critter. Isn't he cute? Can I keep him? Please? Oh please oh please oh please say yes. Please, Mommy?"

Run for our lives! thought Seymour.

I agreed completely.

Unfortunately, the minute the girl felt us start to move, she tightened her grip on our neck.

The little dickens was stronger than she looked. Seymour and I struggled like crazy, but it didn't do much good. After all, we didn't have any teeth, so it wasn't like we could bite her. We didn't have much in the line of claws, either.

How do you protect yourself at home! I thought testily.

Never mind that now! replied Seymour. *Let's get out of here!*

But even when we doubled our effort to break free, we weren't much more effective than a squirming teddy bear.

"Daddy, Daddy," squealed the girl. "Mr. Eyeball Guy is trying to get away! Stop him! Stop him!"

Suddenly we felt something clamp around our neck. "There," said a deep voice. "That ought to take care of him."

A collar! wailed Seymour.

A wave of terror shivered through me. Finally remembering that "Stay calm" was the total content of the first chapter of *Secrets of the Mental Masters,* I tried to push the fear away. It wasn't easy. No one from our group knew where we were. And the people who had captured us thought we were some kind of animal; they had no idea there were not one but *two* intelligent creatures living in this body. Even worse, if our captors were illegal vacationers, they might leave the planet at any time, dragging us halfway across the galaxy.

At the moment it seemed entirely possible we might spend the rest of our lives as someone's pet.

Under the circumstances, staying calm all that easy.

"What a cute critter," cooed the girl, stroking our long blue neck. "I want him to be mine forever, Daddy."

"We'll have to wait and see, Krixna," said the same deep voice. "He's an unusual specimen. I may be able to get a lot of energy credits from one of our customers for a creature like this."

Worse and worse! The girl's father was some kind of interstellar animal dealer. Well, that explained why he had had the collar so handy. He probably had cages around somewhere, too.

I wondered if we were going to have to spend the rest of our lives in a zoo. Suddenly, being someone's pet didn't seem such a bad option.

The guy circled us, eyeing us from all angles. The adult female came over to join him. "What is it, Mir-van?" she asked, putting her hand on his shoulder.

He shook his head. "I'm going to have to consult my reference files for this one, Nanda. It wasn't on the bio-list for this planet, so it must be an import. If so, it's just as well we take it away, before it messes up the ecosystem. The thing is, I can't recall having seen anything like it on *any* bio-list before."

"Well, you haven't studied all of them, silly,"

said Nanda. "The galaxy's too big for even you to do that."

"I know," said Mir-van. "But what if it *is* an undiscovered species?"

If I could only have spoken to him, I would have been glad to explain that since Seymour was actually from Dimension X, odds were good that no planet in our galaxy *did* have a creature quite like him. At least, I would have, until he said, "Think of the price we could get for it *then!*"

"Doesn't he look funny with only that one big eye in his head?" asked the little girl, Krixna. "How do you suppose he eats, Daddy?"

I don't eat, you little idiot, thought Seymour crankily. *My other half does the eating. Then he beams energy . . .*

The thought trailed off, as the terrible truth crashed in on both of us at once.

We had been captured without Edgar!

"Oh, I'm sure he has some way of getting food," said the father with a laugh, not realizing that that was exactly our problem now. "After all, without one, he'd starve to death."

Precisely!

Mir-van snapped a lead line onto our collar. "Come on, boy," he said, starting forward.

We dug in all six heels and refused to move. We shook our eye stalk wildly. All in silence, of course.

"Oh, a stubborn one, eh? Well, I've got ways of dealing with your kind." He bent down and did something to the collar. We felt a strange tingle, then a kind of grogginess that made it hard to think. "Come on, boy," he said again.

It was too much trouble to resist. We went trotting along behind him.

Krixna and her family had camped just outside a grove of weeping trees—close enough so they could hear them, but not so close that the mournful sounds were overwhelming. Next to their camp was a sleek, silver ship, shaped quite a bit like my father's.

"Welcome back!" called a voice. For a moment I thought it was the ship speaking. Then someone waddled around from the far side. He was tall, for an alien, extraordinarily fat, and almost pure white—except for his hair, which was bright green. His face split into a wide grin, displaying several dozen needle-like red teeth. "Ah, I see you've found a new specimen. Strange-looking thing."

Look who's talking, thought Seymour lazily, his mood still affected by the collar.

The fat guy came over to where we stood. Squatting beside us, he ran his hands, which were cool and clammy, over our sides and down our legs. "Feels solid and healthy," he announced. "How does it eat?"

"Don't have the slightest idea," said Mir-van. "But we figure it must have some way."

"I found him," put in Krixna proudly. "He's going to be my pet!"

"Oh, I wouldn't count on that, little one," said the white guy, patting her on the head. "The price this one is likely to fetch is too high for us to let him stay a pet."

"He's mine, Grumbo!" screamed Krixna. "He's mine, he's mine, he's mine!" She threw herself to the ground and began flailing at it with her hands and feet.

Ah, it's "Elspeth: the Sequel", thought Seymour.

Nanda threw a yellow blanket over her daughter. "Pretend she's not there," she said.

"I'll be glad to," said Grumbo, rolling his eyes.

Krixna continued to scream. Everyone ignored her.

Nanda put a hand on her husband's arm. "Are you sure we should keep the creature, Mir-van? I fear it will die if we can't figure out how to feed it."

He shrugged. "If it dies, we'll simply preserve it. Even dead, a specimen this unusual is going to fetch a fabulous price. Alive is better, of course. But—"

"But we'll take what we can get," said Grumbo.

"Precisely," said Mir-van.

CHAPTER
11

"I Still Live!"

GRUMBO TIED OUR LEAD CORD TO A STAKE IN THE
ground. Eventually they all went off to do other
things. Even Krixna got tired of screaming and
climbed out from under the blanket. "See you
later, Mr. Eyeball Guy," she said, giving us a kiss
on top of our eyestalk. Then she went skipping
off, crying, "Mommy! Mommy, I'm hungry. I
wanna eat *NOW!*"

This won't be such a problem after all, thought
Seymour, looking at the stake. *We'll just dig that
thing up and be on our way.*

I figured he was right, until we actually tried
to get near it.

Yow! thought Seymour as we moved toward
the stake. *What's going on?*

Our collar was vibrating and getting hot.

The closer we got to the stake, the worse it felt.

Ignore it! I ordered. *It must be some sort of*

signal coming from the stake that makes the collar do that.

But ignoring the heat and vibrations was easier thought than done; by the time we were about five feet from the stake, the pain was so intense that we had to turn back.

When we turned around, we saw Grumbo grinning at us. "Not bad, little one," he said. "Most creatures who manage to get that close to the transmitter simply pass out."

Then he chuckled and walked away again.

It looks like we're really in for it this time, Uncle Rod, thought Seymour mournfully.

We still live! I replied defiantly. I was quoting, sort of, John Carter of Mars. John Carter is the hero of a series of books by Edgar Rice Burroughs, the same guy who invented Tarzan. Only I like the John Carter books better. Anyway, no matter how bad things got for John Carter he always said, "I still live!"

It seemed like a good motto to keep in mind at a moment like this.

Of course, the John Carter books were just stories. Seymour and I were in real life trouble.

Maybe we can scratch a message on the ground! I thought suddenly.

I don't know how to write, replied Seymour.

Well, I do!

I wasn't sure if the translation program that

made it possible for me to understand the aliens would also let me write their language. Maybe I could only write in English. On the other paw, even if they couldn't read what I wrote, the fact that I was trying to write anything at all ought to prove that Seymour and I weren't just an animal.

It seemed like a good idea. Unfortunately, the ground where we were staked out was covered with about six inches of leaves—not the best surface for scratching out a message. And when we dug a pile of them away, it turned out that the soil was laced over with stiff and wiry roots. Our clawless paw couldn't even make a decent letter, much less a whole word.

Krixna, noticing us, said, "Oh, Mommy! Look how funny Mr. Eyeball Guy is when he digs!"

Yeah, I'm a laugh riot, thought Seymour gloomily.

Later that evening Krixna came over and started petting us. "I love you, Mr. Eyeball Guy," she whispered. "And I'm going to make my daddy let me keep you. I won't let that stupid Grumbo take you away. I won't, I won't, *I won't!"*

As if the very mention of his name had summoned him, Grumbo came waddling over, too. "You did a good job catching this one, Krixna," he said approvingly, patting her silvery hair with a flabby white hand. "I'll see your dad gets you a little present when we sell him."

Krixna made a face, but didn't answer him.

Grumbo squatted down to study us. This made him look pretty much like a dough ball with a streak of bright green mold on top. As he stared at us, a purple line began oozing out of his nose. I thought it was alien snot, until the front end of it lifted up and began waving around as if it was looking for something.

Grumbo put up his finger, and the line began to wrap around it. It was slightly thicker than a toothpick, and about ten inches long.

"Mommy!" cried Krixna. "Grumbo's letting his worm out again."

"Don't fuss, dear," called Nanda from inside the ship. "It's Grumbo's pet, and he can do what he wants with it."

These people are seriously weird, thought Seymour in alarm.

I had to agree.

"Don't you like my noseworm?" asked Grumbo, when he saw us blinking at him. "Krixna doesn't, either. Common prejudice. He's really a very sweet little worm. See?"

With that, he thrust his hand toward us. Most of the worm was coiled around his finger. But the first three inches or so were sticking straight

up. They began weaving back and forth like a snake charmer's snake.

I couldn't be sure, but I thought it was humming.

"He takes up hardly any room," said Grumbo. "And he stimulates my brain in the most wonderful way. I could make a fortune selling these things, if I could only get people to try them. Ah, prejudice, prejudice." He looked at us again, then muttered, "Of course, a worm like this wouldn't do *you* any good, since you don't have a nose for it to live in. You are the weirdest darn critter I ever did see."

Grumbo put his finger back to his nose. The worm crawled halfway in, leaving its lower half dangling over his lip. With a grunt, Grumbo got to his feet and stumped away.

By late that night our separation from Edgar was getting to be a serious problem. What we felt from the lack of energy being beamed into us wasn't exactly hunger—we didn't have a stomach, after all. It was more a dull ache all over our body, and a growing sense of weakness.

I don't know how much longer we can hold out, Uncle Rod, Seymour told me the next morning. *I've never had to do this before.*

Fearful, wondering how much time we had left, I tried to contact Snout again.

No success.

*   *   *

The day wore on. It was hard to tell whether our captors were on Kryndamar for vacation or business. Maybe it was a little bit of both. Whatever the reason, I desperately hoped they were going to stay long enough for our friends to find us.

I can't figure out why they haven't located us already, complained Seymour.

I had been wondering the same thing. But I also knew how hard it can be to find someone who is lost in a forest. One of the neighbor kids had gotten lost in the woods behind our house a few years before I met the aliens, and it had taken dozens of people to find him.

Seymour and I would have only three people looking for us, not dozens. And they would need to cover an area far bigger than the one behind my house. That wasn't even counting the fact that they probably wouldn't split up, for fear of getting lost themselves; certainly Madame Pong wouldn't let Elspeth go off looking for us on her own (though it was equally certain that Elspeth would insist she should be allowed to do so).

So I knew they could easily search for days and not find us.

Besides, it was better to believe that they couldn't find us, than to think that something had happened to them, too.

*　　*　　*

Late that day, while the others were away from camp, Seymour and I heard something that only made things worse: in the distance Elspeth was calling, "Roddie! Seymour! Where are you? Ro-o-o-oddie-e-e-e-e! Seeeeeee-mour!"

A moment later we heard Madame Pong calling, too.

We perked up immediately, as if we had gotten a sudden burst of energy from Edgar.

But the terrible thing was, we had no way to answer them! If we had been free, we would have gone running toward them. But staked down, unable to speak, we could only strain at the cord that tied us, and listen with sinking heart as they went off in the wrong direction, their voices growing dim and distant.

We slumped back to the ground, our despair deeper than ever.

By late that night I feared I was going to have to give up on John Carter's motto. After all, "I still live!" only works while you're still alive—and that condition didn't look like it was going to last much longer for the two of us.

We were lying on our side, with barely enough energy to lift our eyeball from the ground. The others had gone to bed, Krixna crying because she wanted us to sleep with her.

"Mr. Eyeball Guy is *mine!*" she wailed. "Mine, mine, mine, mine, *mine!*"

Always nice to be wanted, thought Seymour. His words, weak and thin, seemed to come from a long way away.

I love to be loved, I replied.

Then neither of us thought anything for a while, because it seemed like too much work.

An hour or so later I felt a tiny wisp of a thought come drifting over from Seymour.

Sorry you had to be here for this, Uncle Rod.

Then I knew he was dying.

Which meant that I was, too.

Bitterly, I thought of John Carter again. Then I realized I had missed the point. Using "I still live!" as a motto doesn't make sense if you give it up when things start to look really bad. It only makes sense if you keep fighting until the last second, until life itself is gone. If you give up before that, it was never really your motto at all.

I decided to try one final time to contact Snout. But as soon as I started, I realized I was in no condition to do so. *Not* because I was weak and about to die. I couldn't do it because I was choking on fear.

Stay calm, I told myself, repeating the opening chapter of *Secrets of the Mental Masters* over and over again. *Stay calm. Stay calm. Stay calm.*

Remembering something Snout had taught me,

I envisioned a private place I had created for myself, a kind of mental hideout based on a secret spot on my grandfather's farm that I used to like to go to. I imagined myself there now, imagined myself safe and happy.

To my own surprise, it worked. The horrible fear began to ebb. As it did, I focused my mind on what I had to do now. With all the energy and hope I could summon, I sent out one final message. *Snout. Snout! Can you hear me?*

Anyone?

Please?

Energy gone, hope exhausted, I collapsed into a kind of blackness.

CHAPTER
12

Swapping Stories

"GET THAT EYE OPEN. HURRY. HURRY!"

The voice seemed to come from somewhere in the distance. At first I thought it was someone yelling at Seymour and me, telling us to wake up. Then I felt someone actually pulling on our eyelid. It hurt. I wanted to flinch away, but didn't have the strength.

"Hurry!" cried the voice again.

A sudden flood of light hit us, as whoever was working at our eyelid succeeded in pulling it open.

Yeow! thought Seymour. *That hurts!*

I agreed, in a groggy sort of way. The two of us would have closed our eye again, if we had had the strength. Then our vision started to focus, and we saw something that gave us a burst of energy.

Kneeling in front of us, his lizardlike face only inches from ours, was Snout!

Close behind him, looking anxious, were Madame Pong and Elspeth.

Just beyond them stood our four captors—Mirvan, Nanda, Krixna, and Grumbo. Krixna, wiping her teary eyes and snuffling her bananalike nose, was whispering, "Please don't die, Mr. Eyeball Guy. Please!"

Snout reached behind him. Grumbo waddled up and handed him Edgar, who was swollen to twice his normal size. The poor little guy looked like a furry purple basketball, or maybe a blowfish, since his fur stuck straight out like spines. For a minute I was afraid he was going to explode. Then he went "EEEEEE-E-E-E-E-P!"

Seymour and I twitched as a jolt of energy come rushing into us, so sudden and fast it was as if someone had hooked us up to a giant battery.

"Eeeeep," said Edgar again, only this time it was more of a sigh. He sounded relieved, and I could see he was starting to shrink just a little.

Snout set him on the ground in front of us. For a little while Seymour and I just lay there, letting Edgar beam energy into our eye.

When we were finally able to stand, we trotted over to Snout.

I was afraid I wasn't going to be able to contact you, I thought.

You didn't.

Then how did you get here? asked Seymour.

Grumbo waddled over and squatted in front of us. "My worm picked up your distress call," he said.

Your worm? I thought in astonishment.

Snout spoke the words aloud for me.

"I told you, the worm stimulates my brain in a most wonderful way. In this case, it acted like an antenna, picking up your distress signal. When I heard you calling your friends, I realized we had made a terrible error."

What kind of error?

Again, Snout translated.

Grumbo looked at me as if he couldn't believe I was asking the question. "We hadn't realized you were a sentient creature," he said, sounding just a little angry. "Obviously, we would never have collared you if we had known that. We are terribly sorry."

I realized that I had misjudged him. I had been so upset and angry when they captured us, and so disgusted by Grumbo's brainworm, that I had assumed he was a total villain. But that wasn't true. He was clearly distressed that they had mistaken Seymour and me for an animal.

How come he can't understand us now? I asked Snout.

Snout, not having an answer, put the question to Grumbo.

"I suspect it was the intensity of your need that let my worm pick up your call," he said. "You were broadcasting, so to speak, at a high level. Now that I'm aware of it, I can tell you're thinking. But I can't pick up specific thoughts. It's more like background noise. Static."

Too bad. I had hoped maybe I had finally cracked the communication problem. But if the only way I could get through to someone was by being at the edge of death, I clearly had a way to go yet.

Krixna came over and put her arms around our neck. "I'm going to miss you, Mr. Eyeball Guy," she sniffed. "But I'm glad you're okay."

"No hard feelings, eh?" said Grumbo, patting us on the top of our eyeball. "It was an honest mistake, after all." He turned to Snout and Madame Pong. "Strangest being I ever saw. What planet did you say he was from?"

"We didn't," replied Madame Pong smoothly. "He is a political exile, and would prefer that no one knew he was here."

"Ah, I understand," said Grumbo. "I feel the same way, if you know what I mean. The fewer people who know *we* were here, the better."

Madame Pong smiled. "I see we are in agreement," she said, making a slight bow.

Grumbo bowed, too. As he did, the worm crawled halfway out of his nose to wave *its* agreement.

"Man, that's disgusting," said Elspeth, a hint of admiration in her voice.

"Would you care to share a meal with us?" asked Nanda, stepping forward. "We feel dreadful about the misunderstanding. Of course, we can't feed your friend here, since he doesn't have a mouth. I don't know what to do to make things up to him."

Just let us go home, thought Seymour.

Madame Pong made another slight bow and said, "Thank you for the invitation. We would be delighted to share food with you."

Which was how we ended up sitting down to supper with the people who had been going to sell Seymour and me for a pet and had nearly killed us in the process. It made me think of that line in the Twenty-third Psalm, the one that goes, "He setteth a place for me in the presence of my enemy." (I had had to learn the whole thing for Sunday school the year before I met the aliens.)

It didn't take Nanda and Mir-van long to come up with dinner, since their ship did all the cooking. Their biggest job was finding out what everyone liked. The two really fussy eaters were Elspeth and Krixna, which seemed to make them feel like they should be best friends.

After dinner Madame Pong told a little story about something funny that had happened to her when she was a kid. Actually, for me the funniest part was trying to imagine her as a kid at all, since that had never occurred to me before.

Grumbo responded with a story of his own. I didn't realize what Madame Pong was up to until I remembered something she had said to me during our voyage to the Mentat: "If you want to know someone, get them to tell you their stories."

That was what she was doing now. Her own story had been a starter, just something to get things rolling. And she had chosen something from when she was little so as not to have to talk about the Galactic Patrol. But Grumbo, no fool, wasn't going to give up too much information, either. So the stories that got swapped back and forth over our campfire tended to be amusing, but not much else.

Until Krixna said, *"I* have a story to tell."

Her mother smiled. "Let the grown-ups talk, dear."

Which made me wonder if kids are treated the same everywhere in the galaxy.

"Oh, let the child talk," said Madame Pong gently. "I love to hear children."

Nanda glanced at Grumbo. He nodded. I guess they both figured that since everyone had been telling stories from their childhood, and since

Krixna was still a kid herself, it would be safe to let her talk.

Krixna smiled triumphantly, her yellow eyes glowing with triumph. "Once, when I was a little girl, we met some giants!"

"Yeah?" said Elspeth, interested, but skeptical. "How big were they?"

"About twice as tall as Daddy!"

Suddenly I was on the alert. It sounded like Krixna's "giants" were about the size of a typical Earthling. (We're considered giants when compared to most of the humanoid species in the galaxy.) I glanced up at the sky. Was it possible Krixna and her family had made a stopover on Earth for some reason? Or—and this was the more interesting thought—had they actually run into some of the lost Atlanteans?

I wished desperately that Dad was with us so he could hear this.

"That's very interesting, Krixna," said Madame Pong with a smile. "And where did you meet these giants?"

"Oh, it was some planet where we had stopped to collect a few specimens for one of our clients," said Grumbo, jumping in a little too quickly to sound as casual as he was pretending to be. "But I'm afraid Krixna is exaggerating just a bit. They were big, but not that big. You know how children are."

"I am *not* zajjeratin'!" said Krixna indignantly. "I always tell the truth, just like Mommy taught me."

I know what you mean, kid, I thought, remembering when I was totally incapable of telling even a tiny lie because my mother had trained me so well.

"Where did you meet these fabulous creatures, sweetheart?" asked Madame Pong again. She was smiling, as if she didn't really believe all this. But I noticed that she directed the question specifically to Krixna, bypassing the adults.

Before the little alien girl could answer Elspeth jumped up. "Eeuuuw!" she shouted, brushing frantically at her arm. "Eeuuuw! Eeuuuw! *Eeuuuw!*"

Madame Pong sighed. "What is it now, Elspeth?"

"I don't know. I just felt something slimy crawl over my hand. Then I . . ."

Her words tapered off.

Her eyes grew wide.

She raised her arm to point. In the same voice you might use to shout, "Fire!" she cried: *"WORMS!"*

CHAPTER
13

The Worms' Turn

NOW THAT ELSPETH HAD POINTED THE WORMS OUT, you couldn't miss them. There were worms all around us, and more squiggling our way from every direction. Hundreds of worms. Thousands of worms. Millions and billions and trillions of worms. The land around us had become a squirming, writhing mass of wormflesh. Utterly silent, they covered the ground like some living blanket. Even as Seymour and I stood staring in horror, we could feel some of them starting to crawl up our legs.

"Mommy!" wailed Krixna. "I'm frightened!"

I probably would have said pretty much the same thing, if I had had a mouth. Elspeth didn't bother with words; she just stood there screaming. Nanda plucked Krixna off the ground to keep her away from the squirming worm horde. Then Mir-van swept Nanda into his arms, to do the same thing. As I saw him standing there, holding his wife who was holding their little girl, it made me wish *my* dad was there. Not to hold me. (Well, maybe I wished for that a little.) Just so we could fight side by side.

Except how do you fight worms? We could step on them. We could tear them away from our bodies. But not all of them. Not even a tiny fraction of them.

I could feel Snout sending a message: *Stay calm*, he urged. *Stay calm.*

But how do you stay calm when you see a writhing flood of worms about to engulf you? They crawled over and around each other, like living spaghetti oozing its way across a plate. Only, unlike spaghetti, the worms were all sizes and colors—from tiny red ones shorter than my little finger to four-foot-long monsters that were brownish purple in color and as thick as a man's arm. And instead of tomato sauce they were covered with gooey slime.

I wanted to run, but it was pointless—the worms were coming from all directions. To run would have been to plunge right into them.

Seymour and I felt more worms oozing onto our legs. We shook our right front leg, sending some of them flying. But as soon as we set it down so that we could shake another leg, it was covered again.

Elspeth was the first to stumble. She disappeared with a scream as the worms flowed over her. Seizing control of our body from Seymour, I started toward her. We hadn't gone more than three feet when I slipped in wormslime and we fell to the ground, too. Instantly, the worms began oozing over us. I could feel a hundred slimy bodies, long and undulating, slither onto our skin.

Gross! moaned Seymour.

Just when I was starting to fear that we would have a problem breathing because of the slime, we got a new surprise.

The worms started to talk to us.

Please forgive our rather frightening way of getting your attention, they said, speaking directly into our head, the same way that Snout sometimes did. *Unfortunately, this was the only way that we could make contact with you.*

By "you" I realized that they meant *all* of us, since it soon became clear that all of us who had been engulfed by the slime were part of the mental link. I could tell because I was picking up our friends' thoughts as well as those coming from the worms.

Yes, we have created a thoughtlink between all of you, confirmed the worms. *Or, to be more precise, we have pulled you into* our *thoughtlink. Our apologies for the fact that the only way to do this was to immerse you in slime. We know it is not the favored tactile sensation for most of you individually brained creatures.*

Individually brained? I thought. I could sense several others, including Grumbo and Elspeth, asking the question at the same time.

That seems like the best term for it, thought the worms. *We worms have to link together in order to gain the capacity for thought. But you creatures think all on your own. It's very efficient, we suppose. But it also seems terribly lonely.*

Being linked to their brains, we could tell what they meant. They were not simply sending us words, or even images; we were connected to their feelings and their memories. This was beyond the kind of brain link I had with Snout when we were communicating. It was more like what had happened in Dimension X when the Ting Wongovia did a mindprobe on me. It was as if we had become part of the worms . . . and the worms a part of us. My mind was filled with images of tunneling, and of sweet, rich soil that suddenly seemed more appealing than a chocolate cookie. I had a sense of generations of worms, a history of wormhood extending behind me into the distant past.

One worm alone was not much to speak of, but their collected minds made a powerful thing indeed. And, in the same way that when people speak they have a tone of voice, the worms' thoughts seemed to carry a sensation of dark and dampness, of enclosed spaces beneath the soil. Yet I could also feel something big about their thoughts, as if their joined senses took in more information than any single mind ever could.

We know everything that happens in Krynda-mar, said the worms, as if responding to my impression. *We know why the trees weep, and where their roots go to drink. We know on what patches of land the rain falls, and where the soil is thirsty. We know each place where the sun is rising, and even better, we know what happens in the darkness.*

Why have you come here now? asked Madame Pong.

I could understand the question as surely as if she had spoken it aloud.

We came because we thought we were called, replied the worms.

What do you mean?

We sensed a great cry of distress, from someone in trouble.

Oh, great, Rod, thought Elspeth. *You're the one who brought the worms!*

What could I say . . . or think? I knew she was right.

On the other hand (something the worms didn't have) I wasn't sure having the worms arrive was such a bad thing. Disgusting? Absolutely. But it was sort of interesting, too.

For one thing, they were clearly able to do what I had been trying to learn—make mental contact with others.

In fact, I had made contact with them!

Alas, we wish we could have come more quickly, thought the worms. *But to gather enough of us to make the link takes time. And now it seems our help was not really needed. Even so, we do have some information that may be of use to you.*

What kind of information? asked Madame Pong.

You have an enemy on Kryndamar.

The jolt of fear and surprise I felt at this announcement was intensified by the fact that everyone else was feeling it, too.

Stay calm! ordered Snout.

Who is this enemy? asked Madame Pong.

The one who stays in the water, answered the worms.

Quat? asked Elspeth. I could tell it really bothered her; she had liked the water guy ever since he fed her that bouncing pickle-thing.

That is the one.

Why is he our enemy? asked Madame Pong. And though she didn't say it out loud, I could tell that she had suspected him all along.

He has been sent here to spy on you, replied the worms.

Who sent him? I thought, dreading the answer.

We do not know. But we have seen him watching you when you do not think he is around. He hides in the pond near your camp and listens to what you say. He seems frustrated because he cannot tell what goes on between the purple being with the pointy face and the blue being with two minds.

How do you know we have two minds? I thought—thereby foolishly giving up any chance I might have had of convincing them we didn't.

We didn't know, until we brought you into our link. After that, we couldn't help but be aware of it. We find it amusing. We are many bodies, joined to make one mind; you are two minds, joined in a single body. It must be difficult.

You can say that again, thought Seymour.

Madame Pong spoke up. Or thought up. Whatever. Anyway, she asked the worms if they would help us.

Normally, we do not like to get involved in the affairs of others, replied the worms. *But this creature, this Quat, we do not like. He pretends*

122

to be pleasant when he is with you. But he is different on his own. He does not respect the land or the water. He is cruel in his behavior. We will help you if we can. What do you have in mind?

Madame Pong told them.

CHAPTER
14

The Spy

THE NEXT AFTERNOON ELSPETH WAS WALKING UP AND down the beach, muttering, "Oh, me, oh, my. Oh, this is such a mess. What am I going to do? They're not doing the right thing. I wish I had someone to talk to about this."

She would do this for a while, then sit down on the sand and snivel for five minutes or so. Then she would get up and start again.

On the third time Quat rose out of the water and came to stand beside her.

"What's the matter, young one?" he asked sympathetically.

Elspeth turned on the faucets. "I just don't know what I should do," she said, tears streaming down her face. "I think we should talk to someone, but they won't let me."

"Talk to someone about what?" asked

Quat, sounding deeply concerned, and very friendly.

"C-c-c-come with me," said Elspeth, sounding as if she were about to burst into sobs. "I'll sh-sh-sh-show you."

Without waiting for Quat to answer, she took him by the hand and led him toward the trees.

The rest of us were there, waiting—including the worms.

Elspeth and Quat hadn't gone more than three steps into the forest when the worms made their move. They dropped from the trees by the thousands. Thousands more squiggled up from the ground. Within seconds the waterman was buried under a writhing mass of wormitude.

The rest of us were already linked with the worms. This meant we were covered with slime, of course. But it also meant that as soon as Quat was pulled into the link, we could sense his thoughts. For safety, the worms put a block in front of our thoughts, to keep them from Quat.

No need for fear, the worms told him now. *We simply want to talk to you.*

Rather than reassuring Quat, this seemed to double his terror. At first I thought this was simply because getting a message from the worms was such a weird thing that it had scared him. But then I picked up one of the waterguy's underlying thoughts and felt a surge of terror myself.

The thought I picked up was this: *What will BKR do to me when he finds out about this?*

My worst fears were confirmed. Quat was not just any spy. He was a spy working for BKR!

Snout, who remained calm, began the questioning.

We have brought you into this link because there are some things we need to learn, he told Quat. *I suspect I already know the answer to the first question, but I want to have it confirmed. Who are you working for?*

I can't tell you that! thought Quat in terror. At the same time another part of his mind was throbbing, *BKR! BKR! BKR!*

With the power of the wormlink, it didn't take long to get the whole story out of him.

I have been working for BKR for many years. I happened to be near Planet Mentat when BKR was last there, along with another of BKR's agents, each of us in our own ships. The boss contacted us, saying he was about to leave on an urgent mission and that he wanted us to watch the planet for two ships, the Ferkel *and the* Jean. *If either of them left, we were to follow and report to him.*

My comrade followed the Ferkel. *That was the last I heard of him. As for me, I followed your ship to Kryndamar. Once I saw where you were landing, I came down myself—not on land, but in water. When I had brought my ship as close as I could, I left it and swam to where you were. Once it became clear that some of you were going to stay on Kryndamar while the ship went elsewhere, I contacted BKR to ask for further instructions. He told me he would get someone else to trail the ship, and that I should stay and watch you.*

So the fact that Quat had been there to save Seymour and me on the morning we were nearly swept out to sea had not been mere coincidence after all. I found myself in the strange situation of feeling grateful to him because he had saved our lives, while at the same time hating him for the reason he had been there to do it.

Have you been in contact with BKR often? asked Snout.

I report in every third day.

Other information floated to the surface of Quat's mind as well, not in direct answer to the question, but stirred up by it. So even without asking, we became aware that when BKR had realized my body no longer contained an active brain, he had been furious.

He had not, however, destroyed my body in a fit of rage, as I had feared he might. He was holding on to it as bait.

To my horror, I soon discovered that he had one more bit of bait in mind.

What is BKR doing now? asked Snout.

Quat fought to hold the information back. But the simple act of asking the question made it rise to the surface of his mind, where it was available to all of us in the wormlink.

He is heading for Earth.

For what reason?

He is going to kidnap the mother of Rod All-bright. BKR hopes that once he has her, it will bring her son out of hiding.

I felt as if I had been hit by a bolt of lightning. *We've got to do something!* I thought.

Got any great ideas? asked Elspeth.

Normally, I would have thought she was just being a smart aleck. But because we were in the wormlink, I could tell she really wanted to do something, too. She just didn't know what.

Unfortunately, neither did I. *We have to go after them somehow*, I thought. *Try to get there first.*

That would be easier if we had a spaceship, pointed out Seymour.

I wanted to scream (but couldn't, of course). I wanted to hit something—though the only thing I would have hit at the moment would have been the worms, who were our friends. Then the answer hit me. *Quat has a spaceship! We can use his.*

I felt a terrible wave of fear from Quat at the suggestion. I didn't care. My mother's life was at stake; probably the lives of the twins, too.

Where is it? I thought fiercely. *Where's your ship?* The worms relayed the question for me.

The answer came as an image of a spot on the ocean floor. That shouldn't have surprised me, since he had told us he had landed in the sea (in which case it probably should be called "watering" rather than "landing") and since he was an underwater kind of guy. But somehow I had assumed he would have moved the ship onto dry ground by this time.

If his answer made sense, it was also disturbing. How deep was the ship? Could any of us swim down to it? We sure couldn't send Quat down to get it—he would just climb in and fly away.

We got Quat to give us more specific information about where the ship was. Then we ended the wormlink so that the rest of us could talk without Quat being part of the conversation.

Madame Pong thanked the worms for their help.

You're quite welcome, they replied. *We always like having someone new to commune with. We learn a lot that way.*

Then they all crawled away.

Unfortunately, they left a great deal of slime behind.

129

"This is disgusting!" said Elspeth, pulling her hand away from her arm and looking at the loop of sticky goo that came with it. She began wiping at her arms. But you couldn't wipe the stuff away. When you tried, it just sort of spread around and got grubby. "Yetch!" said Elspeth.

I agreed. But I was also relieved (and surprised!) that she managed to wait until the worms were all gone to express her disgust. They were really helping us out, and we didn't want to offend them. Only that kind of thing didn't usually stop Elspeth. Again, I wondered how much effect Madame Pong was having on my cousin.

The worms that had been clinging to Quat stayed until last, making it impossible for him to run away.

Grumbo and his group had watched all this from outside the wormlink, not being eager to reenter it themselves. Krixna was standing next to him, holding Edgar, who we had decided should probably stay out as well. Now Mir-van came over to help Snout tie Quat to a tree.

"You aren't going to leave me here, are you?" asked Quat, his voice thick with panic.

"Why not?" asked Snout.

"I'll die! I have to get back into the water."

Grumbo sighed. Taking something from his belt, he pressed it against Quat's neck.

The waterman slumped against the tree.

"What have you done?" cried Elspeth.

"Tranquilizer pad," said Grumbo, extending his hand to show the flat metal square he was holding. "Standard equipment in my business. Don't worry, he'll wake up in an hour or two. In the meantime, we can carry him back to the shore and pour water on him every once in a while."

Snout grabbed Quat by the feet; Grumbo took his arms. As they started back out of the woods, Snout said, "Do you have any diving equipment in your ship?"

"Afraid not," said the pudgy alien. "Why do you ask?"

"We need to retrieve the ship of this spy," said Snout, "and it is hidden underwater." He sighed. "I suppose I shall simply have to swim for it."

It's a cinch we can't, thought Seymour—a private thought, now that we were no longer part of the wormlink.

He was right, of course, as we had learned that first morning when we tried to swim. Even so, I wished he hadn't mentioned it. I hate not being able to do things.

As it turned out, getting Quat's ship wasn't going to be as complicated as we had feared. It was submerged only a few hundred yards offshore, and Grumbo had a little inflatable boat he was willing to let Snout borrow. All he would have to do was row out and dive straight down. All of us, both our group and Grumbo's group, gathered on the beach to watch.

"Don't worry about the dive," said Snout, just before he climbed into the boat. "Breath control is one of the first things they teach you at the Mentat."

We watched as he rowed out to the spot where we believed the ship was located.

Despite his assurances, I felt nervous. But he was right. It wasn't the dive we needed to worry about.

It was whatever was attached to the huge fin I suddenly spotted slicing through the water behind him.

CHAPTER
15

Bargaining

MADAME PONG SAW THE MENACING FIN AT THE SAME
time I did. "Snout!" she cried. "Look out!"

He was too far out and couldn't hear her.
Calmly, still facing away from the approaching
danger, he began to unfasten his cloak.

He dropped it behind him.

Next came his flying belt.

The fin was getting closer.

Madame Pong and Elspeth were both screaming now. "Snout! Snout, don't go in!"

The rising wind blew their words back into
our faces.

The great fin had almost reached the boat.

Snout climbed onto the edge, about to dive in.

SNOUT! I thought desperately. *WATCH OUT!*

Suddenly Snout spun around.

The creature bearing down on the boat reared its
head from the water. Its jaws were nearly as long

as the boat. It had eyes like lanterns, teeth like swords. The long, fishlike body surged forward.

Snout dove into the bottom of the boat. I wasn't sure why, until I saw him go shooting straight up into the air. He had grabbed his flying belt. With no time to strap it on, he had activated it and was now holding it with both hands.

The creature lunged up to catch him. Though its body surged some thirty feet up from the surface, it never left the water completely. As it crashed back into the waves, I wondered how big it really was.

Snout continued his heavenward streak, flying so high we lost track of him.

Well, the others lost track of him. I found myself seeing with his eyes. I had done it! I had opened the mental circuit between us.

Stay calm, Snout! I thought.

All right. That's probably a ridiculous thing to think to someone who is clutching a flying belt that is dragging him straight up, while in the sea that lies increasingly far below there waits a giant creature eager to eat him. Still, it was the best advice I had.

Snout actually laughed in response. *A good point, Deputy Allbright, and one I will try to keep in mind. In the meantime, congratulations on finally being able to make contact with me. And my thanks, as well. You saved my skin!*

As he thought this, he was struggling to get the belt around his waist, where he could control it better. This was a little like trying to wrestle with a flying snake, and he was flopping around in the sky, sometimes looking up, sometimes looking down. His vision, superimposed on mine, was making me stagger with dizziness.

Meanwhile, the creature that had attacked him had turned its attention to Grumbo's boat. It bit it in half, then spit out the half in its mouth as if it tasted terrible.

Suddenly Snout managed to get the belt around his waist. Buckling it on, he came zooming down, straight toward the seabeast.

What are you doing? I thought.

I want to see if I can scare it! replied Snout.

He couldn't. Rather than turning and swimming away, the creature lunged out of the water again, snapping its jaws. Snout turned and shot back toward the sky, out of range of those great teeth.

Suddenly I saw another figure go flying toward the beast. It was Mir-van. He was holding a gun of some sort, and when he got close enough, he gave the beast three blasts. It roared in anger, stretched out of the water, then fell forward with an enormous splash.

"Well done, partner," murmured Grumbo, who was standing next to me.

"Is it dead?" asked Elspeth. She sounded almost disappointed, which I could understand. We wanted the beast out of the way. But it was magnificent, and it would be sad if it had had to be killed.

"Merely tranquilized," said Grumbo. "Much like our friend Quat over there."

I glanced in the direction he was pointing. If I had had a mouth, I would have gasped. Quat was gone.

"Drat!" said Grumbo. "The dose I gave him must not have been strong enough! Or maybe we shouldn't have put him where the water could wash over him. It probably revived him more quickly. That's what I get for being soft. Where do you suppose he's gotten to?"

The question was answered soon enough. The water out where Snout had been fighting the beast began to bubble and change color. An instant later a spaceship erupted from the surface. It soared into the sky, disappearing into a tiny dot even as we watched.

Quat had gotten away, and taken our means of transportation with him.

Grumbo's response when we told him we wanted to use his spaceship was to laugh.

"This is a matter of life and death," said Madame Pong.

"Not mine," replied Grumbo.

If we still had status as members of the Galactic Patrol, we could simply seize the ship, thought Snout, who was standing next to me while Madame Pong and Grumbo argued.

We could seize it anyway, I replied.

True, agreed Snout. *Of course, I was speaking in legal terms to begin with. Just because you can do something under the law doesn't mean you actually can do it, if you know what I mean. And even if we could convince Madame Pong to misrepresent us as still being members of the Galactic Patrol, I doubt Grumbo would give up the ship without a fight. Not sure we could win it.*

In fact, Grumbo soon got a fight. But it came from an unexpected direction. About five minutes into the discussion, Nanda stepped in front of Grumbo and said to Madame Pong, "Are you telling me that the reason you want to use the ship is to save this being's mother?" She was pointing at me and Seymour.

"Yes," said Madame Pong, who had already said exactly that about fifteen times.

"Mr. Eyeball Guy's mommy is in trouble!" yowled Krixna. She started to cry. Tears streamed from her yellow eyes. Silvery snot bubbled at the end of her bananalike nose.

Mir-van picked her up. "Don't cry, honey," he said soothingly. "We'll take care of it."

"Grumbo, you heartless cad," said Nanda, "how can you ignore the fact that this being's mother is in terrible danger?"

"His mother is not my business!" roared Grumbo—which only made Krixna weep all the harder.

"What is your business?" asked Madame Pong slyly.

Grumbo glanced from side to side, as if afraid someone else might be listening. "We deal in rare creatures," he said. "As you well know."

Madame Pong smiled. "How would you like to go to a restricted planet? You'll find creatures there you can't get anywhere else. They have a lovely thing called a cat. Very unusual. It ought to fetch a fine price from the collectors you do business with."

A greedy gleam blossomed in Grumbo's eyes. The noseworm crawled halfway out and lifted its head, as if listening more intently. Even so, Grumbo was not so easily won over. "We don't need *you* to go to a restricted planet," he pointed out. "We can do it any time we want, if we're willing to risk arrest and massive fines."

"Ah, but that's the point," said Madame Pong. "In exchange for a ride, I can offer you diplomatic immunity."

Grumbo snorted. "Easy enough to say. Why should I believe you?"

Madame Pong reached into her pocket and pulled out a ring. With our extraordinary vision, Seymour and I could see, even from where we stood, that it was identical to the one she had given me, the one we still had stowed in our gear.

She handed the ring to Grumbo. He examined it for a moment, then smiled. "Madame, I retract my skepticism. You operate at a higher level than I had realized. Even so—"

"Even so nothing!" said Nanda. "We're going, and that's that."

Grumbo shrugged. "As you can see, I am a prisoner to the whims of my partner's family. All right, we'll take you to this planet."

He made it sound like he was doing it totally against his will.

But the greedy gleam in his eye was brighter than ever.

We packed and left within the hour. Before we went, Snout showed me a small device, a black sphere about the size of a baseball. "If the others come back while we're gone, they'll be able to detect this," he told me. Twisting the top, he spoke into it: "Gone to pick up a friend; back as soon as possible."

That's not very clear, I thought to him.

Don't want to be too specific, he replied, tossing the sphere into the bushes. *It's always possible it might fall into the wrong hands.*

Once we were in space, I was again faced with the weird reality that even though we were traveling faster than most Earth scientists thought possible, it still *felt* terribly slow. I wanted to be home instantly, to make sure that Mom and the twins were all right, and to get them away from danger.

Which was why the week that followed was the longest of my life. I paced the halls of Grumbo's ship, muttering and cursing to myself until Seymour finally said, *Do you suppose I could go somewhere else to live for a while?*

Sorry, I replied—and went right back to my fussing.

Snout spent hours trying to teach me new ways to stay calm. None of them worked. I was half insane with fear and anger and worry.

To make things worse, I had had to agree that once we got there, I would not go into the house. After all, the reason BKR wanted my mother was to use her as bait. And what did he want to catch with this bait? Me!

So I was going to have to wait somewhere else while they went to get her.

* * *

We hopscotched across space, zipping in and out of other dimensions to make the journey faster. The real question, and the one we had no way to answer, was "How far from Earth is BKR?" When we had left the Mentat, we had gone *toward* Earth. If Dad's suspicions had been correct, BKR had gone *away* from it. So despite his head start, he had farther to travel. But *how* much farther? And *when* had he started?

It was like running a race where you had no idea when your opponent had started, or where he was coming from.

"There is nothing about the situation that can be changed by worrying," said Snout.

This was absolutely true.

Unfortunately, it did nothing to stop me from worrying.

I did get a kick out of going into the ship's storeroom to see the strange animals that Grumbo and Mir-van had collected to sell and trade. Almost every time I went there I would find Elspeth and Krixna playing some game. The two of them seemed to get along very well.

At last we were there. Zapping out of a dimensional leap, we saw the blue sphere of Earth floating in space ahead of us.

"What a lovely planet," said Nanda.

"It is," murmured Madame Pong. "Troubled,

but lovely. It has been a special interest of mine for some time."

The planet grew larger in our viewscreen, the continents and oceans rapidly becoming more distinct.

Before long we could see the features of the land, the mountains and rivers, the forests and valleys.

Home! sang something deep within me. *Home!*

Elspeth stood beside Seymour and me, resting her hand on our neck.

"Look, Rod!" she said. "I can see your house!"

The very fact that it was still there filled me with hope. I longed to drop down this instant, to burst inside and call out to my mother and the twins.

But, of course, I couldn't.

We soared past the house, down to the swamp that lies behind it. In the distance I could see the woods where I had always liked to play. The trees were blazing with autumn color. That was a shock. It had been summer when we had left to search for my father. Despite all that had happened since then, it seemed as though things should have stayed the same here at home.

We were traveling at reduced size, which made it easier to escape detection. After a little zipping around through the swamp, we found the spot I had been looking for—an old platform that some duck hunters had built in a tree and then abandoned years before Mom and Dad had built our house.

The wood of the platform was rotted and crumbling, but plenty solid enough to hold Seymour and Edgar and me, since we were only about an inch high.

"We'll be back as soon as we can," said Madame Pong as we climbed out onto the platform.

What she didn't say, what neither of us said, was that if anything went wrong, if they couldn't come back, then Seymour and Edgar and I would almost certainly die here.

But we all knew that it was better for me to die than for BKR to get his hands on what was inside my brain.

Which was why I was once again wearing the ring Madame Pong had given me—just in case BKR *had* gotten to Earth first.

The night was cool. Nanda, fretting, gave us a blanket.

Edgar nestled against Seymour and me, eeeping nervously. Hunkering down onto the platform, we watched as the ship flew back toward the house.

CHAPTER
16

Mom Is Not Amused

THE ONLY THING THAT MADE THE WAITING BEARABLE
was that Snout and I kept our mental connection.
That way I could at least be aware of what was
going on.

This let me watch as Snout did a quick bioscan of the house, and feel enormously relieved
when he said to the others on the ship: "I detect
three large life-forms inside. All indications are
that it is Mrs. Allbright and the twins."

Go on in! I thought urgently. *You've got to get
Mom and the twins and get out of there. Every
moment counts.*

Stay calm, he replied. *We've already worked
this out.*

Indeed, we had had a long debate about how to
make the initial contact while we were traveling.
Going down to meet Mom at two-inch size

would make the landing party harder to detect, should anyone be looking for them. But it would also leave them vulnerable to hawks, cats, or anything else that might want to try eating them.

On the other hand, going to the door at full size could create all sorts of problems if anyone, Earthling or alien, should happen to show up before they got inside.

Crashing through the window, which had been Elspeth's preferred method, seemed unnecessarily dramatic, and likely to scare Mom and the kids.

Finally we had decided that the simplest thing to do would be to enlarge Elspeth, and let *her* go knock on the door.

Since this put her momentarily in charge of things, Elspeth had thought it was a terrific idea.

The others could easily have ridden in her pockets, of course. But we wanted to get Grumbo's ship inside the house, to reduce the chances of it being seen. So they planned to wait in the apple tree until Mom and Elspeth had a chance to open one of the windows at the back of the house.

Through Snout, I fretfully watched the ship's viewscreen as Elspeth approached the front door.

What if Mom wasn't home? Sure, Snout's bioscan had found four life-forms. But maybe there was someone besides Mom in the house—a babysitter or something. I didn't think I could stand the suspense of waiting for her to return if she wasn't here right now.

The call of a nearby bird startled me, reminding me that I was still out in the swamp, not actually in the ship.

I refocused my attention.

The door opened. It *was* Mom. She cried out in astonishment when she saw Elspeth, then threw her arms around my cousin. But at the same time I could see she was looking beyond Elspeth—looking for me. Her face was haggard and worn, and I had a feeling she had not slept well since I left.

Nothing is without consequences, Snout whispered in my mind. *Even good actions carry a price.*

The ship's exterior microphone picked up Elspeth's voice saying, "We have to get inside quickly, Aunt Jean."

They hurried in and closed the door, leaving me wishing that Snout had X-ray vision.

Grumbo waited approximately two minutes, then flew to the back of the house. Mom and Elspeth were just opening the kitchen window. The ship flew through the window and landed on the kitchen counter.

Through the viewscreen, Snout—and therefore Seymour and I—could see the twins standing beside Mom, clinging to her dress. Linda, also known as Little Thing One, was jumping up and down with excitement. Eric, also known as Little Thing Two, had his thumb stuck in his mouth and his eyes open so wide I was afraid they might fall out of his head.

I could tell they had grown since I had been gone, and it made my heart hurt—not the fact that they had grown, but the fact that I had missed it happening.

Grumbo extended the ramp, and Snout and Madame Pong walked down onto the counter.

"Where's Rod?" cried Mom. "Has something happened to him?"

"Roddie!" cried the twins. "Where's Roddie?" Then Little Thing One squinted her eyes suspiciously. "And where's Grakker?" she asked.

Madame Pong put her hands together in front of her. Making a slight bow, she said, "Greetings from the stars, Mrs. Allbright."

She spoke in English, which startled me. I had gotten so used to hearing Standard Galactic I had forgotten about the language implant that made it possible for me to understand it.

Madame Pong started to say something else. Before she had gotten two words out of her mouth Mom cut her off, saying, "Where's Rod?"

I blinked. I think it was the first time I had ever heard her interrupt someone.

"Rod is waiting for you," said Madame Pong,

her voice still calm and gracious. "For reasons too complicated to explain at the moment, it was not wise to bring him into the house."

"Is he all right?" asked Mom. She sounded desperate, and frightened.

"The story is a long one," said Madame Pong, sidestepping for the moment the issue of how "all right" I was. "We will be glad to share it with you in full detail a little later. Right now, you and the twins are in imminent danger. We need to remove you from the house at once."

Mom's eyes widened. "What kind of danger?" she asked, pulling the twins closer to her.

"BKR is after you. Please, I must insist that you get in the spaceship. All will be explained as soon as possible. But we want to get you away from here without a moment's delay."

Mom looked around uncertainly. She had no one to consult with, no one to ask for advice. Finally she sighed and said, "All right, we'll go with you."

"We're goin' on a spaceship!" cried Little Thing One. "Yay for the spaceship!"

"Yay for the spaceship!" echoed Little Thing Two.

"How long are we going for?" asked Mom.

"That is hard to say," replied Madame Pong.

Mom turned pale. "We'll need to pack."

"We can manufacture everything you need on the ship," said Madame Pong. A note of urgency was creeping into her voice.

Mom thought for a second, then said, "Eric, Linda—run and get your teddy bears."

Little Thing One and Little Thing two scurried out of the kitchen. "You can't manufacture those," Mom explained, with a note of smugness. "Not with the proper amount of loving wear and tear." Then her eyes widened. "The dog! We can't leave the dog!"

Madame Pong sighed. "We can bring the dog with us."

Bonehead came bursting through the door about thirty seconds after Mom had called him. Then Grumbo used his ship's shrinking ray to bring Mom, Elspeth, the twins, and the dog down to the proper size for the ship.

"Beam me up, Scottie!" cried Little Thing One, which made me wonder how much TV she had been watching while I was gone.

It took only a few seconds for them to fly back out to the swamp. They landed on the platform where Seymour, Edgar, and I had been waiting.

Inside the ship Madame Pong put her hand on Mom's arm and said, "I must warn you, Rod is not quite as you last saw him."

Mom frowned. "What do you mean?"

"Just come outside, and you'll see," said Madame Pong.

Grumbo lowered the ramp.

Mom followed Madame Pong down the sloping surface, onto the rotting wood of the duck blind. "Where's Rod?" she said.

Seymour and I stepped out from behind the leaf where we had been hiding. Madame Pong stretched an elegant hand in my direction and said softly, "For the time being, Rod is sharing this body with his friend Seymour."

"Are you serious?" screamed my mother. "I let my son go off with you on some insane trip into space, and you bring him back like *this!?!*"

I had never seen her so upset. I was actually afraid she might hurt Madame Pong. With an effort, she got herself under control. "You're joking, aren't you?" she said, her teeth clenched.

"Nope," said Elspeth, helpful as ever, "that's Rod!"

My mother shrieked and dropped to her knees in front of me. "Rod, is it really you?" Her eyes got wider. "He doesn't have a mouth! Why doesn't he have a mouth?"

What is it with this mouth thing? thought Seymour. *You'd think you couldn't live without one. By the way, I think she's sort of my mom now, too. Isn't that interesting?*

I didn't answer him. My attention was all on

my mother. I stared at her as hard as I could, thinking, *It's me, Mom. I'm all right. I'm not happy about this, but I'm all right. I missed you. I love you.*

I'm not sure why I was doing that; I knew I couldn't get the words across to her. But I think it really did have some effect, because she got a little calmer. Tears still running down her cheeks, she put her hand on her chest and closed her eyes. "It's Rod," she said, choking on the words. "It's Rod."

Mother's intuition, I guess.

She extended her hand, placed it gently on our neck. I could feel her fingers trembling.

"My poor Roddie," she murmured. Then she whirled on Madame Pong and shrieked, "What have you done, and how are you going to fix it?"

Madame Pong spoke calmly. "Mrs. Allbright, we deeply regret what has happened to Rod. However he sacrificed his body—which we still hope to regain—in a heroic attempt to save his father's life."

Mom gasped, and I could actually feel her stagger. "You found Art? Where is he?"

"At the moment, he is off trying to regain Rod's body."

"Regain it from where? Who has it?"

"It's a long story," said Madame Pong. "Why don't you come back inside the ship, and we'll see if we can explain it. It would not be good for us to stay here any longer than necessary. There is still the possibility that we may be intercepted by the enemy."

My mother looked around nervously. "Come on, Rod," she said. "Let's go inside."

Man, it's like I'm not here at all, thought Seymour peevishly.

Give her a chance to get to know you, I replied as we climbed the ramp.

Grumbo was sitting on the floor, playing with Bonehead. "Fascinating creature," he said as we climbed back into the ship. "Is this one of those cats you were telling me about, Madame Pong?"

"You talk funny!" said Little Thing One, who was sitting on the floor next to Grumbo. "I can't understand you."

"And he has a worm in his nose!" cried Little Thing Two. He turned toward Grumbo. "Show Mommy your worm! It's gross. I almost barfed."

"That's nice dear," said Mom, sounding totally distracted. She turned to Madame Pong. "All right, let's hear the story."

But before Madame Pong could begin, a voice came over the ship's speaker system.

"This is the Galactic Patrol. Identify yourself, and prepare to be boarded!"

CHAPTER
17

Disgrace

"You promised us diplomatic immunity!" said Grumbo, glaring at Madame Pong. He looked both furious and frightened.

"So I did," said Madame Pong, nodding her high-domed yellow head. "I expect to fulfill that promise, too. But I cannot achieve that status for you magically. I have to present myself to these officers and explain the situation."

Grumbo settled down just a little. He glanced at Mir-van, who was standing with his arm around Nanda's waist. They both looked nervous, but Mir-van nodded, as if to say it would be all right.

"What's going on?" asked Mom. She sounded really worried.

"Good news, actually," said Madame Pong, switching to English for a moment. "It appears the Galactic Patrol had another ship here to guard you after all—though why they didn't intercept us earlier, I am not certain."

"This is the Galactic Patrol!" said the voice over the speaker again, sounding impatient, even angry. "Identify yourself and prepare to be boarded."

"Verify that it really is a patrol ship, Grumbo," said Madame Pong, speaking in Standard Galactic again. "If it is, then you should do as he asks."

"As if I had a choice," snorted Grumbo. He went to the console and touched a button that I recognized from my work with Phil the Plant; it sends an encoded radio signal between ships, confirming their identity.

Grumbo glanced down at the console. "It's a patrol ship all right," he said wearily. Touching another button, he leaned forward and said, "This ship is the freetrader *Grumbo's Pride,* as you know from our signal. We have come to Earth at the request of Madame Pong, who has high diplomatic status. I am now opening the doors. Enter in peace."

The door opened. The ramp extended down.

A moment later four beings entered the spaceship.

"These guys are weird!" said Little Thing One.

Weird to human eyes, I guess. I had seen enough aliens by this time that these four didn't strike me as being all that strange. Maybe even less strange than usual, since they were all built on the same basic lines as humans (you know: two arms, two legs, two eyes, that kind of stuff). Even so, they looked as different from each other as a collie does from a bulldog. Actually, one of the four looked quite a bit like a bulldog herself, since she had a mushed in face and big hanging cheek flaps. I noticed that she had an interesting looking box strapped to her waist.

The second alien reminded me of Quat, though I couldn't tell if this one was male or female. Its scales were silvery blue, and it wore a suit that was clearly designed to keep it wet.

I couldn't really see the third alien; it wore a hooded cloak, and its face was deep in shadow. All I could see was its hands, which were gray.

The leader of the group wore a uniform much like Grakker's, so I assumed he was a captain. He was tall (for an alien) and thickset, with arms that looked as though he had been working out since before he was born. (Or hatched, or budded, or whatever—you could never tell about that kind of thing with aliens.)

Weird as they were, the aliens' looks didn't bother me. What bothered me was the fact that they had their guns out. This struck me as being unnecessarily hostile. But I suppose it was like cops entering a suspicious building; they had to be ready for the worst.

"Let's see your documents," said the captain, holding out his hand.

He's awfully cranky, I thought to Snout.

No crankier than our Grakker, replied Snout.

You've got a point, I admitted.

Grumbo slid aside a panel in the main console and pulled out some cards. The bulldog woman took them and inserted them in a slot in the box she had strapped to her waist. The box pinged.

"Documents are valid, Captain. But the ship is not cleared for this planet. They may be smugglers, or illegal traders."

"I told you, we're escorting a high-level diplomat!" cried Grumbo, his voice desperate. "Tell him, Madame Pong!"

The leader's eyes widened. "Ah, Madame Pong. I should have realized." He swung his gun back toward Grumbo. "You've chosen a fine one to throw your lot in with, you fool. This woman was indeed a diplomat. Once. She is now a renegade from the Galactic Patrol, and subject to immediate arrest."

"You promised!" moaned Grumbo. His voice was thick with panic and betrayal, and I thought he might start to cry. I felt sorry for him—though I felt sorrier for Madame Pong.

Our diplomat maintained her calm exterior. "You are correct, Captain, that I am in renegade status. However, Freetrader Grumbo had no way of knowing that, and acted in good faith in bringing me here. I ask you to hold him blameless for his actions. I assume you are here to provide protection for Mrs. Allbright and her offspring. Believe it or not, that is my mission, too. As long as you can assure me that they will be well guarded, I will submit to arrest without protest."

"You can protest all you want," said the captain. "It won't make any difference. You know I have no choice in this matter. You are to be arrested."

He gestured toward Snout. "Can I assume that this is Flinge Iblik, who was Mental Officer on the *Ferkel* before the entire crew mutinied?"

"Guilty as charged," said Snout.

"And what is *this?*" asked the captain, pointing his gun toward me.

"That's Mr. Eyeball Guy!" said Krixna, her banana nose flaring with indignation. "Be nice to him, you big meanie!"

The captain actually chuckled. "Is he yours, little girl?"

Krixna shook her head. "He used to be," she said sadly. "But now he belongs to that lady." She was pointing toward my mother.

"Ah, Mrs. Allbright," said the captain, speaking in English now. "Do let me apologize for all the drama and disruption. We are indeed here to watch over you, and we should have intercepted this situation before it even started. For that failure, I offer my apologies." Glancing behind him at the hooded figured, he added, "I will probably also be offering up the career of the officer who failed to detect the situation in time."

"I don't understand what's going on," said my mother.

"Hardly a surprise, under the circumstances. Let me introduce myself. I am Captain Bickler, newly commissioned to the good ship *Merkel*."

So they recovered our sister ship, thought Snout. *That is good news. I hope the crew was all right.*

"It is my task to guard you and your youngest children," continued Captain Bickler. "It is my *hope* to reunite you with you husband and your son. And, alas, it is my unpleasant duty to place these two renegades under arrest."

I thought Mom might point out that she and I had already been reunited, but I think everything was moving too fast for her at that point.

The captain made a gesture with his hand, and the alien who reminded me of Quat stepped forward. It was holding a pair of blue rings. I recognized those rings; I had been forced to wear one myself the time that Smorkus Flinders took over the *Ferkel*. They were like high-tech handcuffs. Except instead of just holding your hands together, they pretty much paralyzed you from the neck down.

As the scaly alien placed the rings over the heads of Madame Pong and Snout, Captain Bickler said, "Flinge Iblik and Madame Pong, I arrest you in the name of the Galactic Patrol for violation of Galactic Ordinance number 432.75.896, Galactic Ordinance number 51.6547.2b, and Galactic Ordinance number 14. You will be tried in Galactic Court, and judged by a team of your fellow officers. May justice prevail."

May justice prevail, thought Snout, speaking to me alone.

Captain Bickler extended his hand to my mother. "If you and the children will follow me," he said. "I will lead you to our ship."

"And the pets," said my mother, who still looked confused and frightened.

The captain nodded. "Of course we must bring the pets," he said. He turned to the bulldog lady and gestured for her to come close. Speaking softly, he said, "Once we're off the ship give that fool Grumbo a good warning, shake him up a bit, put the taste of fear in his mouth. Then let him go."

She nodded, and stood with her arms behind her back, waiting for us to leave.

The scaly guy fastened a pair of leads to the blue rings he had put on Madame Pong and Snout. Each lead had a black box at the other end, about the size of a deck of cards. He flipped a switch on each of the boxes, then gave a tug at the leads. Madame Pong and Snout walked along behind him. I got the feeling they had no choice.

It was weird to step out of Grumbo's ship, into the autumn wilderness of our swamp, and see another ship waiting to take us in. The fact that the *Merkel* was identical to the *Ferkel* made it even weirder. Entering it was like walking into a house that looked exactly like the one you live in, yet knowing that the people you would find inside were not your family, but complete strangers.

Mom kept a tight grip on the twins' hands— which was just as well since there were a lot of holes on that rotting old platform big enough that they could easily have fallen through and disappeared into the swamp.

We climbed the ramp of the *Merkel*. I glanced back at Grumbo's ship, hoping the fat trader wasn't going to get in too much trouble. Then the door closed behind us.

"Well, that's a relief," said Captain Bickler. "I was getting really tired of this costume."

I felt a cold chill. Turning, I watched in horror

as his face began to split down the middle. Slowly, as if something was pushing it from the inside, the whole body separated, opening like a sideways clamshell.

"Ahhh, that's better," said a familiar voice.

Out stepped BKR.

CHAPTER
18

Event Horizon

BKR HAD BLUE SKIN. INSTEAD OF HAIR HE HAD OR-
ange spikes jutting out all over his head. Other
than that, he might almost have been cute, if his
face hadn't been pinched and twisted by his love
of cruelty.

"Well, isn't this lovely?" he said, rubbing his
hands together. "Let's see . . . we've got a nice
selection of Allbrights, two former crew members of the *Ferkel,* and a couple of weird little
animals. We can jettison them later, if we need
to. You and the twins should be enough to flush
your son out of hiding, Mrs. Allbright. I'm quite
confident that he will come in search of you."

He doesn't know! thought Snout, with a wave
of triumph and relief. *He doesn't have any idea
that he's captured you along with the rest of
us, Rod!*

I had just realized the same thing. And the

twins weren't aware of me, either, since I had had my reunion with Mom outside the ship, and we hadn't had a chance to tell them what the situation was. Elspeth could be counted on to keep her mouth shut. Mom was the one I was worried about. She had no idea what was really at stake, didn't have a clue as to what Dad had stored in my brain.

Don't say anything, Mom! I thought, desperately wishing I could actually contact her the way I could Snout. *Don't let him know I'm here!*

She glared at BKR. "What in heaven's name do you want my son for?" she asked coldly.

I felt a surge of relief. She hadn't spilled the beans.

Her glare, which would have stopped me in my tracks, didn't seem to have any effect on BKR at all. "Actually, I've got *most* of Rod already," he said. "But that boy of yours is a clever rascal, and he managed to get away with one important part: his brain."

"What do you mean?" cried Mom, as if this was the very first time she had heard this information.

Oh, well done, Mrs. Allbright, thought Snout. *Keep him off guard.*

I was impressed. This wasn't quite lying, but it was close. I hadn't known that Mom could do it.

BKR smiled. It was clear he had expected Mom to be both surprised and distressed by this news. It was also clear that he was enjoying telling her about it. Which made sense, given that cruelty was his hobby.

Putting his little blue hands together, he said with mock sorrow, "I should be more specific. What Rod got away with was the *contents* of his brain. His brain itself is still inside his body. Alas, it's even emptier than it used to be, and I don't have any idea where the essence o' Rod has gotten to. Perhaps my friend Snout can tell us," he said, walking over to Snout and tickling him under his long, outthrust chin.

Snout said nothing.

Madame Pong spoke up. "How did you get the codes to operate the *Merkel*?" she asked. "Stealing a patrol ship is one thing. Being able to operate it as if it were still part of the patrol is something else altogether."

"That was my doing," said the hooded figure. The gray hands reached up and drew back the hood, revealing a lean face with enormous, multifaceted eyes.

I had seen those eyes before, on Planet Mentat.

"Arly Bung!" said Madame Pong, her voice thick with shock and disgust.

Arly Bung was chief of security for the Mentat. She was also, it was now clear, a supreme traitor, and an enemy of everything the Mentat and the Galactic Patrol stood for.

"Don't be so pious, Pong," said Arly Bung. "After all, we're two of a kind—renegades who have turned against the given order of things. You and your friends rebelled against the Galactic Patrol. I rebelled against the Mentat. Traitors all, aren't we, when you come right down to it?"

That was cruel and unfair. Madame Pong and Snout had gone renegade in order to continue doing the job they had sworn to do. They had done it knowing the cost, accepting the price, for the sake of a greater good. Arly Bung had gone against her oath for—well, who knew what her reasons were? But it sure wasn't for the greater good of the galaxy.

I wondered if she had ever had a code.

A high *ping* sounded from the console.

"Ah," said BKR. "Bonzetta has finished scaring the daylights out of those poor traders."

He opened the door. The bulldog-faced alien came stomping into the ship. She was smiling, which was a fairly terrifying sight. "I disabled their ship," she said. "Then I set them loose in the swamp. You should have seen the weeping and wailing."

"That's rotten!" cried Elspeth. "How could you do such a thing?"

166

My insides hurt at the thought of our friends, who were now only two inches high, trying to survive in the swamp. I could think of several things out there that would consider poor little Krixna just the right size for a snack.

BKR, however, was grinning from ear to ugly ear. "Well done, Bonzetta. I'm sorry I missed it. Now, let's go."

"Go where?" asked Mom, struggling to keep her voice even.

"Oh, to a little place I keep for special occasions," said BKR. "It's a fortress I've built for myself at the center of the galaxy. Interesting location, I think; it rides right at the edge of an event horizon."

"What do you mean?" asked my mother, who was holding the twins close to her sides.

"You've never heard of an event horizon?" asked BKR, in mock surprise. "Really, dear lady, that wandering husband of yours should have talked to you about these things. Ah, men. They just don't communicate the way they should. Money. Emotions. The nature of the universe. They ought to be more open about these things, don't you think? Well, since that foolish Ah-Rit didn't do his job, I'll fill you in. A black hole is quite a lovely thing, a collapsed star—I love it when things collapse, don't you?—a collapsed star with gravity so incredibly powerful that even light can't escape its grasp. Anything that gets sucked into a black hole vanishes forever, squished down to an unimaginably tiny size by the magnificently destructive force of its great gravity. The 'event horizon' is the line you dare not cross, the point at which the black hole's gravity has you and you can't escape. And *that's* where I've built my little hideout—orbiting the black hole at the center of the galaxy, riding just outside the event horizon. It gives sort of a special thrill to every day. Nothing has ever gone wrong, but, hey, you never know. One day there might be a slight miscalculation and *thwooop!*— there we go, sucked right into the black hole! Wouldn't that be fun? Well, unusual at least. Of course, there are practical reasons to be there. If I ever get this little project of mine off the ground, the black hole will provide the power I need to make it work. So, you see, it's not just the romantic in me that had me put my little hideout there. Oh, no no no. It's utterly practical."

Can I go back to Dimension X now? thought Seymour. *I don't like it here anymore.*

"Now, come along, I want to show you something, Mrs. Allbright," said BKR, sounding as if he were trying to sell her a washing machine. "Bonzetta, keep an eye on Snout and Pong. If they make the slightest move, blast them. Don't kill them, of course." He turned to Mom and said with a smile, "I never let anyone die *that* easily. Now, after you, Mrs. A."

Mom, who looked numb, headed in the direction he indicated. The twins, clinging and whimpering, went along after her. So did Elspeth.

You should go, too, thought Snout. *Learn all you can. It's our best chance for surviving.*

So Seymour and I trotted along behind them.

The ship, being built on the same plans as the *Ferkel*, was painfully familiar to me.

BKR led the way to the sick bay—or what had been the sick bay. He had ripped out the healing lamps and replaced them with some devices of his own. In the center of the room were three containers. Each had tubes and wires running into the bottom, and a crystal clear top.

Inside the first container, still as death, like Snow White in her glass coffin, lay Phil the Plant.

Inside the second floated Grakker.

Inside the third, achingly close yet impossible to reach, was the thing I wanted most in all the world.

My body.

CHAPTER
19

Time to Choose

WITH A SCREAM MY MOTHER FLUNG HERSELF ONTO the case.

"My baby!" she cried. "What have you done to my baby?"

I wasn't sure if she was really that upset over seeing my body like that, or if she was faking for BKR's benefit. Either way, it was kind of embarrassing.

"Oh, do calm yourself, Mrs. Allbright," said BKR coolly. "The truth is, I've taken quite good care of dear little Roddie. In that stasis tube he will neither age nor change. He's in exactly the same condition he was in when I got him: a good physical specimen, with absolutely zero brain activity. Actually, that seems to be fairly common among you Earthlings. Now, if you do have any idea where the contents of Rod's brain have gotten to, I'd suggest you tell me. After all, you and I actually want the same thing—to reunite your son's mind with his body. We're natural allies, if you think about it."

Mom, still facedown on the container that held my body, shook her head without saying a word.

BKR sighed. "So be it. I had hoped we could do this the easy way. Well, just to be sure you're telling the truth, we'd better test you a bit."

Mom lifted her head from the case. Tears streamed down her face. "What do you mean?"

BKR shrugged. "Surely you can see that I have to be positive you're not holding back any information before we bother to go all the way to the center of the galaxy." He smiled. "Fortunately, we have the twins with us. I think the threat of tossing one of them out of the ship somewhere between here and Mars should get you to tell me anything you know, don't you?"

The blood drained from Mom's face. "You wouldn't!"

BKR's eyes went hard. In a voice as cold and empty as space itself, he said, "Madame, you have no idea what I am capable of."

I heard the echo of Madame Pong's voice from when she first told me about BKR and his cruelty: *Millions have wept.*

BKR pulled out his ray gun. "Now, I think it's time we returned to the main cabin."

*   *   *

The walk back to the main cabin was the longest of my life. Though the thought terrified me, I knew I would give up both my brain and my body to save the twins if I had to. The problem was, it wasn't simply my own life I would have been risking by revealing myself to BKR; it was the life of everyone in the galaxy.

I figured this must be even harder on Mom than it was on me. Even if she knew I was willing to have her give me up, how could she choose between two of her children?

Stay calm, thought Snout. *Stay calm.*

He was right; panic wasn't the answer. The problem was, panic seemed to be the logical response to this situation.

We reentered the main cabin. Madame Pong and Snout were right where we had left them. Two of BKR's henchbeings—Bonzetta and the fishy-looking one—were lounging on chairs. They had their ray guns out, but they seemed very relaxed. Arly Bung was still standing, watching the prisoners with those huge, insectoid eyes of hers.

"Quice, I want to leave the planet," said BKR. "Make it happen."

The alien who looked like Quat sighed and went to the control panel. It fiddled with some dials. The ship rose, and my heart sank.

Elspeth turned to Snout and Madame Pong.

"They've got Grakker and Phil," she said breathlessly.

Snout already knew that, of course, since he had seen it through our eye. But though Madame Pong tried to conceal her response, I caught a fleeting moment of shock and dismay in *her* eyes that told me our Mental Master had not shared this bad news. Which made sense; there was no point in letting our enemies know that he could see what I saw.

"Goodness," said BKR, rolling his eyes. "I forgot to mention that, didn't I? Well, the child is right. One of my people captured your friends before they could make their way back to Galactic Headquarters. Poor Grakker; always such a stickler for rules, and now he's a mutineer. I almost let him go, since it would have been such fun to think of his misery and humiliation when he arrived at Galactic Headquarters. Alas, there was always the chance he would have actually gotten the boneheads that run things to believe him, and messed up my plans. Couldn't let that happen, could we?" He turned to Quince. "How are we doing?"

"We have left Earth's grav-field," replied the fishlike alien. "Do you want me to move into hyper-mode?"

"I *live* in hyper-mode," said BKR gleefully. "But don't take the ship there yet. We have some business to do first."

He went to stand before my mother. The twins were clinging to her sides.

"You're a poopy face!" said Little Thing One.

"We hate you!" added Little Thing Two.

"Such charming children," said BKR. "It seems a shame to have to sacrifice either of them. Oh, well. There's nothing to be done for it. Now, which one shall it be?"

He pointed at Little Thing One and began to recite a rhyme, moving his finger back and forth as he spoke.

> *"Iggitty Biggitty*
> *Boggitty Boo,*
> *Today's the day*
> *I'm choosing you!"*

He ended by pointing at Little Thing Two.

"Oops, too bad!" said BKR with a smile. "You're it! I don't know why I bother, actually, since it always comes out the same way. I knew it would be you before I started. Quince, open the airlock. We have someone who needs to experience the wonders of space."

He picked up Little Thing Two. Immediately Little Thing One launched herself at him. "You let go of my brother, you poophead!" she cried.

My sentiments exactly.

I was surprised, though I shouldn't have been,

when my mother did much the same thing. With a scream that came from someplace so deep inside herself I don't think she had even known it was there, she flung herself at BKR. Elspeth and Bonehead joined the fray as well. So did Seymour and I, though we were hardly built for fighting.

The battle was over in seconds. Arly Bung, Quince, and Bonzetta used their stun ray on poor Bonehead, who had turned into a whirling fury of fur and fang. Then they peeled Mom and Elspeth and Little Thing Two away from BKR, who had been laughing hysterically throughout the entire scene.

"Nicely done," he said when it was all over. "Though I would have expected no less from the wife of Ah-rit Alber Ite."

Mom's eyes were wild. Her hair looked like it had been combed with a blender. Her chest was heaving and her blouse was torn. "You're vile," she said, spitting the words out as if they were poison in her mouth.

"I know," replied BKR with a smile. "Now, let's get on with our business, shall we? Is the inner door open, Quince?"

"Ready as requested, Captain."

Little Thing Two was crying. Elspeth pulled away from Bonzetta's grasp. "Take me instead!" she said defiantly.

"Bad trade," said BKR, shaking his head.

"Then take us both," she said, reaching out for Little Thing Two.

"Now that's not a bad idea!" said BKR. "Doubles the stakes. I kind of like that."

Elspeth ignored him. She had Little Thing Two in her arms and was trying to quiet him, whispering that everything was going to be all right.

There is more to your cousin than we have suspected, said Snout in my head.

You're not kidding, I replied.

Elspeth carried Little Thing Two to an opening on the far side of the cabin. She looked back at us, took a deep breath, then stepped in.

The door closed behind them.

BKR turned to my mother. "You have thirty seconds, Mrs. Allbright. At the end of that time you either tell me where Rod's brain patterns have been stored, or we will open the outer door, and *whooosh!*, out go the brats, sucked into the vast emptiness of space. Take your time, dear. You have twenty-one seconds left."

He began counting.

Mom looked around frantically.

Come on! I thought to Seymour.

We ran over to stand beside her. But how could I get the message across that I *wanted* her to tell him where I was. I knew she was hesitating because she didn't think he would really do something so awful.

176

I also knew she was wrong. He *would* do it.

"Five," said BKR. "Four. Three. Two."

"Wait!" said Madame Pong and Mom simultaneously.

"Ah," said BKR, turning to Madame Pong. "Another country heard from. And pray, what do you have to tell us, Pong?"

"Rod's brain patterns are stored in the belly of the little blue creature standing next to Mrs. Allbright."

BKR burst into hysterical laughter. "You'll have to do better than that, Pong!" he said. "You expect me to believe such a ridiculous story?"

"It's true!" cried my mother. Tears were streaming down her cheeks. "It's true. It's true!"

"Ladies, you insult me," said BKR. "The count is one, the count is done. Quince, open the outer door. Let the brats eat vacuum!"

CHAPTER
20

Journey to the Center of the Galaxy

"NOT SO FAST," SAID A NEW VOICE.

We all turned in surprise. Well, all of us except Madame Pong and Snout; they couldn't move, because of the blue rings.

It was Selima Khan. She had stepped out from behind a panel in the wall of the room. She had a ray blaster in each hand, and a don't-mess-with-me look on her lizardlike face.

"Get away from that control panel," she said to Quince.

When the scaly alien seemed to hesitate, she punctuated the order with a shot from the blaster in her right hand. The red ray passed directly over Quince's head, missing it by about two inches.

"Make any move except directly away from

that panel, and the next shot will be lower," she said softly. At the same time she fired a shot with her left blaster. Arly Bung hissed in pain, and dropped her ray gun.

"Drop yours, too, Bonzetta," said Selima Khan sharply. "And move it, Quince!"

The water-breather glanced at his boss. BKR nodded. Quince backed away from the panel.

"Now open the inner door, Mrs. Allbright," said Selima Khan. "I'll tell you which button to push."

Mom went to the control panel and did as Selima Khan directed.

The inner door slid open. Elspeth and Little Thing Two came hurtling into the room, straight to my mother's arms. She caught them up and held them close, crying softly into their hair.

"Care to tell me what you're doing on my ship?" asked BKR. His voice was calm, but you could sense the fury seething beneath it.

"Not until you and your gang are under control," replied Selima Khan. "Elspeth, take the blue rings off Madame Pong and Flinge Iblik. Put one on BKR, the other on Arly Bung. We'll tend to Bonzetta and Quince when we have a chance to look for more rings."

Elspeth moved to do as Selima Khan requested. She had just lifted the ring from Madame Pong's head when a hideous orange creature came roaring into the room.

I recognized him at once; it was our old enemy, Smorkus Flinders.

Selima Khan turned and fired at him with both ray guns. One shot went wide, the other struck him on the shoulder. Smorkus Flinders howled in pain, but continued straight at her, knocking her to the ground.

The ray guns flew out of her hands and went skittering across the floor. Quince snatched at one. Elspeth hurled herself at the other, but Arly Bung got it first. Bonehead, barking like a maniac, attached himself to Smorkus Flinders's foot. The orange monster shook his leg, sending the poor little dog flying against the wall. He yelped as he struck it, then fell silent. Edgar, eeeping like crazy, scrambled onto BKR's back, then onto his head. With a cry of rage BKR ripped the chibling away. I heard an awful tearing sound—some of the orange spikes that grew from BKR's head had gone with Edgar, leaving finger-sized holes behind. An ugly purple fluid was oozing up from the holes. If BKR felt any pain, he ignored it. Flinging Edgar to the side, he held out his hand to help Smorkus Flinders to his feet.

"It's about time you showed up," he snarled. "If your nap had lasted any longer, we might have all been dead."

Smorkus Flinders shrugged his lumpy shoulders.

"You're not," he said gruffly. "So don't whine about it."

I was the one who felt like whining. Thirty seconds ago we were in control of things. Now the enemy was on top again. And he wasn't going to let his guard down twice.

"Slap them in suspended animation," said BKR. "All of them!"

"We don't have enough pods," said Quince. It sounded nervous.

"Well you can skip the animals, you fool," said BKR. "And the twins, if necessary. Now get busy!"

"Yes, your nastiness," said the scaly alien. Then he and Arly Bung and Bonzetta hustled us all down to a lower level of the ship, where they proceeded to put everyone except Edgar, Bonehead (who had survived his collision with the wall), and Seymour and me into Sus-An pods.

At first I wondered why BKR didn't simply jettison us "animals," as he had threatened to do with Elspeth and Little Thing Two. After a while, I realized there were two reasons. First, he figured he might be able to use us at some point for emotional blackmail; I knew this because I heard him explain it to Bonzetta. Second, it simply amused him to have us around, because we gave him something new to be cruel to. This one I had to figure out on my own, but it wasn't hard, since he kicked Seymour and me every time he happened to see us—kicked us, and then laughed.

Poor Bonehead was having a hard time because he couldn't go outside to pee and stuff. Since he knew he wasn't supposed to make messes on the floor, he would hold it until he couldn't stand it any longer, then let go with a rush. I had been worried about what would happen the first time BKR found a puddle of piddle, but as it turned out, the ship's cleaning robots immediately took care of any messes the dog made. The first time one of them came scuttling out behind Bonehead to take care of one of his "accidents", it nearly scared the little guy to death. Even so, I was relieved.

Despite the fact that no one yelled at him for going inside, Bonehead still didn't like it, and whenever he had to do his business he would stand by a door and whine, hoping for someone to let him out. Poor little guy had no idea that going outside would mean instant death.

I wasn't totally alone during this time, since I had Seymour to keep me company. That I had expected.

What I hadn't expected was Snout. But he had contacted me soon after BKR had ordered everyone put into suspended animation.

Rod, are you there?

We're here, I thought excitedly. *Where are you?*

My body is in the Sus-An pod, just as BKR ordered. But I beat him to the punch and moved myself into trance state before the pod was activated. This let me shield my mind from the pod's effects, so I could stay in contact with you.

Great, I replied. *Do you have any suggestions?*

Stay out of BKR's way as much as you can. Yet at the same time, stay near him when possible. The more you can learn, the better off we'll be.

It was a strange journey. I was on the ship of my enemy, wandering freely, face to face with him every day—and yet he had no idea I was even there, because he thought I was just some silly creature he was keeping around in the hope that I might prove useful.

At least once a day Seymour and I slipped into the room where my body was stored. I would stare at it longingly, imagining myself back inside it, aching to feel my own skin, use my own hands and legs. Would I ever get it back?

I might have gone wild with worry if Snout hadn't continued to work with me on the training we had started back on Kryndamar, teaching me more about mastering my thoughts and focusing the power of my brain.

Actually, it's my brain, Seymour pointed out, more than once.

So what's your complaint? I would reply. *You're learning, too, aren't you?*

For all the good it will do me, he responded gloomily.

Be cheerful! urged Snout.

Are you nuts? thought Seymour. *We're prisoners on a ship owned by a madman, and everyone we care about is in the deep freeze. I'm not sure that qualifies as a laugh riot!*

We still live, I would think—though I wasn't all that cheerful myself, when you came right down to it.

And then one day we were there. As we approached the center of the galaxy, Seymour and Edgar and I went to stand on the main deck, so we could watch on the ship's viewscreen. What we saw was a circle of absolute blackness. I had expected that—it was a black hole, after all. What I hadn't expected was the ring of shimmering light that surrounded it.

Those are light rays that have been trapped by the black hole's gravity, explained Snout. *They are in orbit around it.*

Since I had been taught that light always travels in a straight line, the idea of light being in orbit really weirded me out.

The universe is vast and strange, said Snout.

Sooner or later most of the rules we think we know are broken.

BKR's fortress was in orbit beyond the ring of light. The fortress was big, about the size of a large supermarket. A door opened in the side of it, and he steered the ship into a landing bay. We docked against a sealed opening.

"Home at last," said BKR as the doors between the ship and the fortress opened. He sounded satisfied, almost happy. "What a view we have of that vastly powerful pit of destruction. Cozy, isn't it, Bonzetta?"

"If it's so cozy, then perhaps you won't mind taking a little nap," said a familiar voice.

A very familiar voice.

My father's.

A red canister came hurtling into the ship. It burst open, sending out a cloud of white gas. At the same time the doors between the ship and the fortress slid shut again.

"Curse you, Ah-rit!" screamed BKR. Grabbing his throat he began to stagger, gasping and choking.

Groggy, thought Seymour. *Can't keep the eye open.*

As we began to fall asleep, I saw Bonzetta yawn and slide to the floor. Arly Bung slumped in her chair. Smorkus Flinders toppled sideways.

"No!" screamed BKR. "NO NO NO NO NO!"

186

But his cries were getting weaker, and soon he was flat on the floor.

That was the last I saw for a time, because we were asleep, too.

When Seymour and I started to wake, traces of the white gas still floated in the air.

The others were still asleep.

How long have we been out? I wondered.

Just a couple of minutes, replied Snout, who was still connected with us.

How come we woke up so soon? asked Seymour.

I suspect the effect of the gas was reduced because you breathe through your skin, answered Snout.

The door slid open, revealing two figures. Even though their faces were covered by gas masks, I knew it was my father and Tar Gibbons. Seymour and I scrambled to our feet, eager to go and greet them.

Dad held up a small sensor of some kind. When it made a clear, high tone, he turned and nodded to the Tar. They slipped off their masks. Dad stepped through the door.

To my horror, no sooner had he crossed the threshold than a beam of red light shot across the room.

Dad cried out, and slumped to the floor.

Tar Gibbons spun to see where the light had come from, as did Seymour and I.

Quince was sitting against the wall, eyes wide open, ray gun in hand.

"That stuff doesn't work so well on someone who's breathing water," said the scaly alien. "Now, crouch down and put your hands on your head, bugman. Do it fast, or I'll change the setting on this ray gun and do something permanent to your friend on the floor there."

Tar Gibbons did as Quince ordered. In only a moment the water breather had a blue ring around the Tar's neck.

In that same moment our last hope had collapsed in ashes.

No, thought Snout. *There is still one thing we can do.*

What? I asked desperately. *What hope do we have left?*

We have you, Rod. I can channel your brain back into your own body. Once you have control of it, perhaps you can turn the tables once again, and let us get the upper hand.

But if I fail . . .

If you fail, BKR will have your brain, and with it the information he needs to carry out his fiendish plan to destroy time itself.

Could I really risk the fate of every living being in the universe in order to save my friends and family? *Well, I've still got Madame Pong's suicide ring,* I thought. Then I realized that the ring wouldn't be any use if BKR captured me once I was back in my own body, since it would still be on Seymour's paw!

But there was something else to consider. Even if we did manage to keep the information in my brain away from BKR, who could tell what new scheme he might cook up to terrorize the universe next year, or the year after?

Would anyone *ever* have a better chance to stop him than I did right now?

The dice were mine to roll.

At stake—the fate of the universe.

CHAPTER
21

Transfer Student

BKR HAD MY BODY TRANSFERRED TO A ROOM IN HIS fortress. He sent the animals—Bonehead, Edgar, and Seymour and I—along with it.

Then, one by one, he brought the others out of suspended animation, and took Grakker and Phil out of the stasis tubes.

One by one, he had them searched for weapons, then marched to the same room.

It should have been a joyful reunion—joyful for the crew, and even more joyful for my parents, who were seeing each other for the first time in more than three years.

But there could be no joy while we were in the grip of BKR. And very few words were spoken, because everyone knew BKR would be listening.

My father was the last to enter the room. When

he did, my mother gasped and ran to him. She threw herself into his arms, and they held each other tight.

"Who's that man?" asked Little Thing One, tugging at my mother's skirt.

"Do we like him?" asked Little Thing Two.

My father closed his eyes, and his face was lined with pain.

"Yes, dears," said Mom softly. "We like him. We like him very much. Even though he does have some explaining to do."

"Why are you crying, Mommy?" asked Little Thing One.

But Mom shook her head, and wouldn't—or couldn't—talk anymore.

After a minute Little Thing One went over to the case that held my body. "Roddie!" she said, patting the clear top. "Roddie, wake up!" She turned to my mother, her lip trembling. "Why won't Roddie wake up?"

"Roddie's not there, Linda," whispered Mom. "That's just his body. The rest of Roddie, the real Roddie, is somewhere else."

"Where?" demanded Little Thing Two.

"Alas," said Madame Pong quickly, "that is a great mystery." It was one of her classic absolutely-true-but-totally-empty-of-information answers—given, I was sure, for the sake of BKR.

"Well, I want him back!" said Little Thing Two. *"Now!"*

"We all want Roddie back," whispered Mom. "But not now. Not here. Now come sit with me, and be quiet."

Mom and Dad sat on the floor and the twins climbed into their laps. I longed to join them, but didn't dare, for fear it would tip BKR off to where I was hiding.

After about an hour of this uncomfortable silence, the door opened. Quince, Bonzetta, Arly Bung, and Smorkus Flinders came in, holding their weapons raised and ready to shoot. They ordered us to stand together in the center of the room.

When they were satisfied, BKR came through the door.

"Well, well, well," he said, rubbing his little blue hands together. "Isn't this nice? Friends and family, all in one place." His smile faded, and when he spoke again his voice was cold as ice. "Now look, you people. I am convinced that at least one of you knows what has happened to Rod Allbright's brain, and I intend to get that information out of you no matter what it takes. Is that clear?"

"Perfectly," said Madame Pong, speaking for the group.

"Good. You have an hour to think about it. When that hour is up, you will be brought to the main control room of the fortress. I think you'll like it up there; we have a nice view of the black hole, and you can observe that magnificent pit of destruction quite clearly. The nothingness is quite stunning. I'm going to leave you here until then. No need to bind you—the doors will be sealed, and there's nothing in here you can use as a weapon. When we return to the main deck, either you tell me what I want to know, or one of you goes out the air lock while the rest of us watch. And then another . . . and another . . . and—"

He paused, and tipped his head to one side. "The only thing I haven't decided yet is whether the lucky first place winner should enter the greater universe *without* a space suit, so he or she will die quickly, or *in* a space suit, so that he or she will still be alive as he or she gets sucked into the black hole." He made a little clucking noise. "Decisions, decisions. They're the curse of a thinking man's life. Well, see you in a little while, kids. Happy pondering!"

With that, he and his guards left the room, sealing the door behind them.

"Now what do we do?" asked Mom when they were gone.

"We wait," said my father. At the same time he

grabbed his earlobe and wiggled it, to remind Mom that anything we said was being listened to.

She nodded and fell silent.

I repeated her question to Snout, glad for once that the only way I could communicate was in a way BKR could not hear.

We wait, he replied, echoing my father. *We think. We stay alert for any opportunity. And we stay calm.*

Seymour and I padded over to look at my body. Putting our little blue feet on the front end of the stasis tube, we stared down into my face. It was weird to be outside my own skin, staring in, so close I could have touched it, and yet somehow impossibly far away. After a moment Madame Pong and Snout came over to join us.

"I miss that boy," sighed Madame Pong. "I wish I knew where he was."

The tiniest hint of a smile poked at the corners of Snout's mouth. *BKR won't believe she really means that,* he explained. *Even so, it should help keep him guessing.*

Soon, far too soon, BKR and the others returned. They put blue restraining rings on everyone except Bonehead, Edgar, and Seymour and me.

Then they led us all to the main deck. On a huge viewscreen we could see the black hole in all its destructive glory.

"Now here's another vexing question," said BKR once everyone was in place. "Shall I start big, or small? For example, I could begin with Mrs. Allbright, or maybe one of the twins; either choice would pack a very solid emotional punch. On the other hand, I might want to save the big stuff for later. I could start with the dog, I suppose—kind of as a small sample of what's to come. Plus, he annoys me, so I would be killing two birds with one stone, so to speak. The problem with that is, you might get used to the idea, build up some tolerance for it. No, we should definitely start big."

He broke into a broad grin. "Problem solved! See, you just have to think these things through carefully. So, we've decided that it will be someone you all care about a lot. But who? I need someone who will make an impact, but who is not apt to take the information I need with her. One of the twins would probably qualify. But I've already tried that once, and I do so hate to repeat myself. There's no art in it, if you know what I mean."

He shrugged. "Well, then, that settles it. By the way, you don't mind my thinking out loud like this, do you?"

No one answered.

"Good. Anyway, the choice is . . . ah, I can see you're hanging on my every word. Thank you. I do so love an audience."

"Just get on with it, BKR," growled Grakker.

Even in these terrible circumstances, it was good to hear his cranky voice again.

BKR rolled his eyes. "You never did have a proper sense of ceremony, old chum. All right, since you insist, the winner is . . . Mrs. Allbright!"

"No!" cried my father.

"Mommy! Mommy!" cried the twins.

Something in my heart seemed to snap in two.

My mother straightened her shoulders. She looked around the room, letting her gaze rest first on Dad, then the twins. She didn't look at me for more than an instant.

Finally she spoke.

"I do not believe *any* of us know where Rod is," she said, lying more fluidly than I would have thought possible. "But even if we did, it would be my deepest prayer that not one of us would tell you, no matter what you do."

She turned back to my father, gazed at him with tears trembling in her eyes. "I have waited three years for you to come back, Art. I never expected that when we met again, it would be like this. You kept things secret from me, dear-heart, more secrets than you should have, with reasons that I think were much too small. Now we have a reason much greater. If you love me, if you ever loved me, if you love the children we created together, do not breathe a word to this little beast."

BKR rolled his eyes and clapped his hands lazily together. "Oh, very good, Mrs. Allbright. Very good indeed. Now, are you nearly ready to go?"

And that was when I made my choice.

NOW! I thought to Snout. *Transfer me NOW!*

It began. I could feel myself being funneled out of Seymour, as if I were being sucked out of something by a psychic vacuum cleaner. The world swirled around me. I experienced a great wrenching, as if my brain was being torn in half, then a terrible emptiness.

Good-bye, Uncle Rod! called Seymour. *I'll miss you!*

Thoughts and memories and emotions swirled around me, a weird combination of images of my old life and thoughts of the adventures I had shared with Seymour, memories of Kryndamar and Krixna tumbling over images of the swamp behind my house, and my fifth-grade classroom.

And then it was over, and I was in my own body again.

Did you ever come home after a long trip? Then you know how it feels to be back in your own space, with your own things, after being away for too long. Coming back to my own body was a little bit like that, but in a way so deep that I can't begin to explain it.

I lay there for an instant, feeling almost sea-sick. Then I realized I had no time for that. I had to get out, to get to my mother.

I tried to move.

To my horror, I was held tight by the stasis tube.

I had my body back, but I still couldn't use it! I was frozen in place.

And BKR was about to fling my mother into a black hole.

CHAPTER
22

Me at Last

I THOUGHT I WAS GOING TO EXPLODE WITH PANIC.

Stay calm, said a familiar voice. I was relieved to find Snout was still in mental contact with me.

But staying calm seemed a ridiculous idea under the circumstances.

What do I do? I thought to him in horror. *I can't get out of this thing. I can't move at all!*

Nor is there any way for me to get out of this room, thought Snout.

Then I heard another voice. *I think I can get away. They're not paying much attention to us animals.*

It was Seymour. He was still in contact with me!

Hey, what's the surprise, Uncle Rod? Two guys share a brain as long as we did, and they ought to be able to talk to each other. Hold on. I'll be there as soon as I can.

I could see what Seymour was seeing. I could see what Snout was seeing. I just couldn't see what *I* should have been seeing, because my eyes were shut, and I couldn't open them.

On the main deck, BKR was strutting back and forth, spouting off about how he was going to throw my mother out the air lock. At first I wondered why he was going on about it so long.

Two reasons, replied Snout, answering the question even though I hadn't actually asked it of him. *The first is that he wants to build up tension, force us to really think about what he's doing. His hope is that someone will crack and tell him where you are. The thing is, it's unlikely to change the situation even if we do. If someone breaks, BKR will probably send us all out the air lock anyway, just for the fun of it. Which brings up the other reason he's blathering on right now: he's enjoying the fear and pain on everyone's faces, the hurt and terror in their eyes. He wants to savor the moment as long as he can.*

Millions have wept, I thought, quoting Madame Pong again.

Precisely, replied Snout.

I probably would have wept, too, if I could have forced my body to do *anything.*

Still watching through Snout's eyes, I saw BKR stop in front of my mother.

"We're going for the suit," he said decisively. "It will be more scientific that way, don't you think?"

"Scientific?" echoed Mom. She sounded numb, as if the horror of the situation had gotten so out of hand she could no longer feel it.

"Well, of course, dear lady. If we simply chuck you out of the ship, you'll be dead long before you fall into the grip of the event horizon, and we won't gather a scintilla of data regarding how it feels to be sucked into that giant gravity pipe. What a wasted opportunity! But if we pack you into the suit, why, we can listen to your reaction. Probably nothing but a lot of screaming and moaning, of course, which will be boring when you come right down to it. But you never know until you try. And it will probably affect the children quite intensely."

Mom straightened her shoulders. "I thought nothing came out of a black hole," she said. Her voice was hoarse, weary.

BKR smiled. "Mrs. Allbright, you are too quick for me. You're right, of course. Mere radio waves couldn't make it out at all; they'd be sucked right in with you. That's why I'm going to keep you physically connected to us, for a while at least. Oh, I'm so proud of this little bit! You see, I have about twenty thousand miles of ultra-fine cable to which I am going to connect you. Though the cable will be lost to us forever once we've reeled it all out—a pity, but one must sacrifice if one wants to do science properly—until it goes, we'll be able to monitor your words. Or noises. Screams. Whatever. Oh, I would dearly love to keep track of you for the entire fall. Who knows what wonders you may experience? Odds are you'll be dead within minutes, of course. But maybe not! Good gracious, I do envy you this adventure, dear lady. Consider the possibilities! What if the black hole really is a gateway to another universe? What if your body actually does withstand the terrible forces that will be pulling it, extending it, stretching it so that it's miles long? It probably won't, of course. But there's so much we still don't know. Wouldn't it be fascinating if you did survive? It makes me want to weep that we won't be able to follow your progress all the way down."

Keep talking, you creep! I thought. *Keep talking!*

BKR was so wound up in his little speech, in trying to terrify Mom and the others, that he didn't even notice Seymour slipping out of the room.

"Now, Mrs. Allbright, if you'll just step into this suit."

Hurry, Seymour! I thought desperately. *Hurry!*

Through Snout's eyes I could see Mom approach the space suit that BKR had offered her. She stopped, turned, looked toward my father, toward the twins.

Simultaneously, through Seymour's single eye, I could see the corridor rush past as he galloped down to where my body lay waiting.

"I love you, Art," said my mother softly.

"Come, come, Mrs. Allbright," said BKR. "This is no time for sentiment. There's science to be done here. Unless, of course, any of you care to tell me where Rod's brain patterns have been hidden."

"We don't know!" said Mom defiantly. What she was really saying, of course, was "Don't tell him. I've made my choice."

And I've made mine, I thought. *Now if I can only follow through on it! Hurry, Seymour! HURRY!*

Stay calm, thought Snout. *Prepare yourself. Remember the Warrior Science you have learned from Tar Gibbons. You will need all your skills once you are free.*

Mom began stepping into the space suit.

Seymour came skidding into the room. I could see myself through his eye, see my body floating in the stasis tube.

Now what? he thought. *How do I get you out of there?*

I don't know! I thought desperately. *Pull the switch. Push the button. Just get me out!*

But through his eye I could see a bewildering array of buttons and switches all around the base of the stasis pod.

Stay calm, Rod, thought Snout. *If you keep calm, you can let me see what Seymour is looking at, and I can help you. Panic, and it will disrupt the flow of information from him to you to me.*

I tried to empty myself of fear, of any thought at all, to make myself a clear tube so that the images could flow through me, from Seymour to Snout. I tried to imagine myself in my secret place, but my mind, frantic with concern for my mother, kept pulling me back to the moment and the urgent need to get out.

I can't do it!

You're generating negatrons! thought Snout. *You have to stop, or you will never be able to break free.*

I can't! I replied.

You must! Remember the things I taught you, Rod. Calm yourself. Calm yourself.

Panic fluttered like a bat through the chambers of my mind. Cold terror lurked behind me, whispering of my mother's death.

Let go, I whispered to myself. *Let go, Rod.*

I envisioned my secret place again, remembering how I used to go hide there when I was younger, when life was simpler, before I had met these aliens and found out the truth about my father. I began to examine it in tiny detail, remembering all the things I loved about it—the feel of the grass, the smell of the air, the sound of the wind rustling around me.

And suddenly I was free. I could move. I flexed my fingers in astonishment.

I had my body back! I wasn't simply inside it, it was mine to use again.

Reaching up, I pushed against the crystal lid that covered me.

It wouldn't move.

New panic surged through me. *Stay calm!* whispered a deeper, wiser voice—not Snout this time, but actually some part of me.

Seymour, I thought. *Find the latch. Get me out of this thing.*

Through Snout, I could see that my mother was now fully suited up. BKR was guiding her to the air lock.

I can't find a switch! thought Seymour.

There's only so long you can stay calm. A wave of fury swept through me, and I began to pound against the crystal lid. That was useless, stupid.

Then I caught the rage, caught it and channeled it, as the Tar had taught me to do what seemed a lifetime ago. "Will you let the anger devour you, or will you devour the anger?" he had asked.

"Do not throw your power away. Focus it, my *krevlik*. Focus it."

I caught the anger. I channeled it, funneling all my rage at BKR, and all my fury at what he had done to me and my family, into one mighty thrust. Pulling my feet back, slamming upward, I sent the lid of the stasis tube flying.

All right, Uncle Rod! thought Seymour.

I knelt and took the ring from his paw. "See you later, buddy," I said, as I slipped it onto my finger. Then I bolted past him, out the door.

Well done, Rod, thought Snout. *But don't forget yourself. It will do no good to burst in here unarmed!*

He was right, of course. In my rage I had been ready to do just that, as if I could have somehow fought off BKR and his thugs barehanded.

I headed for the weapons room, which I had found when Seymour and I were exploring the fortress. I grabbed two blasters from the wall and tucked them into my belt, then grabbed another pair, checked their loads, set them on megastun, and headed out of the room.

BKR was guiding my mother into the air lock when I got there. "I want to be with her when she goes out," he said to the others. "Just in case she has a little secret that she wants to whisper to me. Don't worry, Mrs. Allbright; I'll be able to hear you. I'll be wearing a suit of my own, of course. Only mine will be attached to the wall, so I don't get sucked out into space."

I wanted to burst into the room, both guns blazing. I wanted to shout, "Beware the wrath of Rod Allbright, you alien scuzzball!"

It would have felt great. But odds were good that if I actually did it, Arly Bung and the others would blast me before I could get within ten feet of BKR.

So I pressed myself to the wall, and inched forward until I could peek around the corner of the door.

All eyes were focused on BKR and Mom—including those of the guards.

I took a deep breath, centered my strength, tried to remember everything the Tar and Snout had taught me. A bit of Warrior Science came to mind, and I slid silently to the floor.

Then I fired both ray guns at once.

Arly Bung and Quince dropped like bricks. Smorkus Flinders and Bonzetta spun at the sound. Two more blasts from my ray guns, and they were flat out, too.

Now it was just me and BKR.

Except he didn't know I was there. And though every fiber of my being wanted to rush into the room and shout my defiance and my anger at him, I slid backward.

Good boy, thought Snout. *Let him come to you.*

"What's going on there!" screamed BKR.

No one answered.

I had pulled back so far I couldn't see into the room. But I was still connected to Snout and Seymour. Through their eyes I could watch BKR. My great fear was that he was going to use my mother as a shield. If I had burst into the room, I know he would have done exactly that.

But my silence, my pulling back, did the trick. He was furious and frightened.

And he forgot to stay calm.

Flinging my mother aside, he started toward the door.

I slithered back down the corridor, around a corner. Still on the floor, I pressed myself against the wall.

BKR darted into the hall. Once he left the room, he was out of sight of Snout and Seymour, so I couldn't see him, either. But I could hear him—hear him coming down the hall, cursing in his fury.

I wanted to leap out, to face him, to grab him and shake him until he snapped.

I wanted him to see me, to know that I, Rod Allbright, the "pudgeboy" he had tormented back when he was disguised as an Earthling, was the one who was defying him, the one who was going to stop his evil plans.

But I waited.

I kept still.

I stayed calm.

And then he was there, looking around the corner, looking at eye level for someone standing there to fight him.

"Beware the wrath of Rod Allbright," I whispered from my spot on the floor.

Then I blasted him with the ray gun.

CHAPTER
23

Homeboy

THE VOYAGE HOME WAS A BITTERSWEET TRIP. IT TOOK about a week, and as we traveled, I transferred several times from ship to ship, traveling about half the time in Dad's ship, and half the time in the *Ferkel*.

BKR and his gang were in Suspended Animation in the *Ferkel* and would eventually be delivered to Galactic Headquarters for justice.

"Probably go back in Sus-An after the trial," was Grakker's prediction. "Except for Smorkus Flinders. He may get sent back to Dimension X. Be a stupid thing to do, but the way the court works these days, you can never be sure."

There would be another trial, too—a trial for the crew of the *Ferkel*, who were still considered renegades.

"I suspect it will come out fine," said Madame Pong, trying to reassure me. "We will probably be put on probation and have letters of censure placed in our records. That's for the public record. Privately, we may even be commended for finally bringing BKR to justice. The bigger question, Rod, is what to do with you."

What to do with me, indeed.

I am Deputy Rod Allbright of the Galactic Patrol, and crew member of the renegade ship *Ferkel*.

And I *like* being part of the Patrol, like traveling with the crew. It feels good, and real.

On the other hand, I'm only a kid.

And I wanted to go home.

And yet . . . and yet I wondered if I would ever truly be at home on Earth again, or if part of me would always be longing for the stars, and the good ship *Ferkel*, and the crew I had come to love.

The first thing we did when we got back to Earth was go into the swamp to see if we could find Grumbo, Nanda, Mir-van, and Krixna.

To my relief, they were still alive, though fairly frightened, since they thought they might be stranded on Earth as two-inch-high aliens forever. But they had made the best of things, building a shelter for themselves in one of the old willow trees. And Grumbo and Mir-van were having a good time studying all the creatures in the swamp.

Even so, they were thrilled when we showed up with the materials to repair their ship.

"I knew you would come back!" cried Krixna, running over to give Elspeth a hug. (We were at two-inch size at the time, too.)

She looked over at me. "Who's that?" she asked.

"My cousin, Rod Allbright," said Elspeth. "He's a member of the Galactic Patrol. We just got him back."

"I've met you before, haven't I?" said Grumbo, looking at me shrewdly. His worm crawled out of his nose and waved around, as if sniffing at me.

"Yes, sir, you have," I said.

Grumbo glanced at Seymour, then back at me, and I nodded. We didn't need to say anything else.

They were eager to get on their way. But before they went, Grumbo handed Madame Pong a business card. "In case you're ever looking for an interesting pet," he said. Krixna sidled up to Elspeth and handed her an envelope. "This is a picture of me and those giants I told you about," she said. "So you'll know I wasn't lyin'." Then she dropped to her knees and threw her arms around Seymour and whispered, "G'bye, Mr. Eyeball Guy. I'm gonna miss you!"

"Come along, dear," said Nanda. "It's time for us to be leaving."

Then they all climbed into their ship and flew away.

"Soon it will be time for us to leave as well," said Madame Pong the next morning. The crew had spent the night in our house. (They had remained at their two-inch size, so there was plenty of room.) "You will have to make a decision now, Rod."

"I have to stay here," I said, a little sad, but very sure.

Madame Pong nodded. "We will put in an application for leave for you. I'm sure it will be granted with no problem."

"Galactic Ordinance 143.78.92b makes it a certainty," said Grakker gruffly.

We went back out to Seldom Seen, the field behind the swamp behind our house. The crew enlarged the *Ferkel*.

Then, one by one, they came to embrace me and Elspeth.

The two of us knelt, so that we would be about the same height as the crew.

First to say good-bye was Phil the Plant. Putting his leaves on my shoulders, he said, "Fly straight and fly true, Deputy Allbright."

Plink, peeking out from beneath his leaves, squeaked in agreement.

Next Snout wrapped his long arms around me.

"It has been a pleasure to work with you, Rod," he said gently. Then he winked and added, "Stay calm."

"I'll do my best," I promised.

Selima Khan, who had been standing by his side, took my hand. "It has been my pleasure to serve your father during his time in exile," she said. "I believe you are a worthy son to him." Turning to Dad, she said, "Farewell for now, Ahrit. May your heart be at ease."

"Farewell, Selima Khan," said my father, bending down to embrace her. "May you, too, find that which will put your heart at peace."

Snout closed his eyes, and a shadow seemed to cross his face. But he said nothing.

Next to speak was Tar Gibbons. "I shall miss you, my *krevlik,*" said my beloved teacher, stretching its long neck forward and resting its head on my shoulder. "Warrior Science teaches us to rejoice in our comrades, and I have had much joy in your companionship and your courage. You have a Warrior Heart, strong and true. Once again, I release you from your bond to me. Yet this Warrior hopes that we may meet again some day."

"For all you have taught me, my thanks," I murmured. "You will always be my teacher."

Madame Pong had been standing with her arm

216

around Elspeth's shoulder. Now she came to me and said, "As for me, Rod, I think you have the potential to be one of the Galactic Patrol's finest. When you are ready to rejoin us, all you have to do is call." She took my hand in hers and slipped the ring she had given me from my finger. "No need to have this in lethal mode now," she said, deactivating it. She handed it back to me. "Even so, it is a good thing to have. Possession carries certain . . . privileges."

Then she taught me how to use it to send a signal that would eventually reach the *Ferkel,* a signal that would say, "I'm ready."

Clenching the ring, I put my hand over my heart and made a slight bow. Madame Pong tapped her forehead against mine, which I guess is something they do on her home planet.

At last it was Grakker's turn. He stared up at me for quite a while, then finally growled, "If ever I have a ship again, there will be a place in my crew for you, Deputy Allbright."

"There is no captain I would rather serve," I replied.

Grakker nodded, then backed away without hugging me. It wasn't the way he did things.

He said his farewells to my mother and my father and Elspeth, then led his crew into the *Ferkel.* A moment later they started for Galactic Headquarters, taking a piece of my heart with them.

Then it was just us, my family, home again together at last. My father hoisted Little Thing One onto his shoulders. I did the same with Little Thing Two. Then all of us, Mom and Elspeth, Seymour and Edgar, Dad and me and the twins, with Bonehead tagging along behind, walked out of the swamp and back to the house.

Back home.

At last.

About the Author and the Illustrator

BRUCE COVILLE was born in Syracuse, New York. He grew up in a rural area north of the city, around the corner from his grandparents' dairy farm. In the years before he began to make his living as a writer, Bruce had many jobs, including grave digger, toy maker, elementary teacher, and magazine editor. Now he mostly writes, but spends a fair amount of time traveling to speak at schools and conferences. He also produces and directs full-cast recordings of fantasy novels.

In addition to more than sixty books for young readers, Bruce has written poems, plays, short stories, newspaper articles, thousands of letters, and several years' worth of journal entries.

He lives in Syracuse with his wife, his youngest child, three cats (Spike, Thunder, and Princess Ozma Fuzzybutt) and a jet-propelled Norwegian elkhound named Thor.

Some of Bruce's best-known books are *My Teacher Is an Alien*, *Goblins in the Castle*, and *Jeremy Thatcher, Dragon Hatcher*.

KATHERINE COVILLE is a self-taught artist who is known for her ability to combine finely detailed drawings with a deliciously wacky sense of humor. She is also a toy maker, specializing in creatures hitherto unseen on this planet. Her other collaborations with Bruce Coville include *The Monster's Ring, The Foolish Giant, Sarah's Unicorn, Goblins in the Castle, Aliens Ate My Homework,* and the Space Brat series.